THE GOLD AT THE STARBOW'S END

Frederik Pohl

BALLANTINE BOOKS • NEW YORK
An Intext Publisher

SBN 345-02775-2-125

"The Gold At The Starbow's End," Copyright © 1972 by
the Condé Nast Publications, Inc. Originally published
in *Analog*.

"Sad Solarian Screenwriter Sam," Copyright © 1972 by
Mercury Press, Inc. Originally published in *The Magazine of Fantasy and Science Fiction*.

"Call Me Million," Copyright © 1970 by United Publish-
ing & Distributing Corporation. Originally published
in *Worlds of Fantasy*.

"Shaffery Among the Immortals," Copyright © 1972 by
Mercury Press, Inc. Originally published in *The Magazine of Fantasy and Science Fiction*.

"The Merchants of Venus Underground," Copyright ©
1972 by U.P.D. Originally published in *If*.

First Printing: August, 1972

Cover art by John Berkey

Printed in the United States of America

BALLANTINE BOOKS, INC.
101 Fifth Avenue, New York, N.Y. 10003

It was a Grand Plan—even a grandiose plan—the creation of humans whose minds would evolve to something superhuman. The trouble is, no human can imagine what a superhuman will do.

Or what the process by which the human race was condemned might be.

Or what it's like to swallow a jolt of something fine and mellow—like a person.

Or how it feels to be more famous than Einstein.

Or any other unlikely fancy Frederik Pohl wants to turn his mind to—and then it's no problem at all to imagine . . .

All published by Ballantine Books, Inc.

This is an original publication—not a reprint.

Contents

The Gold at the Starbow's End

Constitution One

Log of Lt-Col Sheffield N. Jackman, USAF, commanding U.S. Starship *Constitution*, Day 40.

All's well, friends. Thanks to Mission Control for the batch of personal messages. We enjoyed the concert you beamed us, in fact we recorded most of it so we can play it over again when communication gets hairy.

We are now approaching the six-week point in our expedition to Alpha Centauri, Planet Aleph, and now that we've passed the farthest previous manned distance from Earth we're really beginning to feel as if we're on our way. Our latest navigation check confirms Mission Control's plot, and we estimate we should be crossing the orbit of Pluto at approximately 1631 hours, ship time, of Day 40, which is today. Letski has been keeping track of the time dilation effect, which is beginning to be significant now that we are traveling about some 6 percent of the speed of light, and says this would make it approximately a quarter of two in the morning your time, Mission Control. We voted to consider that the "coastal waters" mark. From then on we will have left the solar system behind and thus will be the first human beings to enter upon the deeps of interstellar space. We plan to have a ceremony. Letski and Ann Becklund have made up an American flag for jettisoning at that point, which we will do through the Number

Three survey port, along with the prepared stainless-steel plaque containing the President's commissioning speech. We are also throwing in some private articles for each of us. I am contributing my Air Academy class ring.

Little change since previous reports. We are settling down nicely to our routine. We finished up all our post-launch checks weeks ago, and as Dr. Knefhausen predicted we began to find time hanging heavy on our hands. There won't be much to keep us busy between now and when we arrive at the planet Alpha-Aleph that is really essential to the operating of the spaceship. So we went along with Kneffie's proposed recreational schedule, using the worksheets prepared by the Nasa Division of Flight Training and Personnel Management. At first (I think the boys back in Indianapolis are big enough to know this!) it met with what you might call a cool reception. The general consensus was that this business of learning number theory and the calculus of statement, which is what they handed us for openers, was for the birds. We figured we weren't quite desperate enough for that yet, so we fooled around with other things. Ann and Will Becklund played a lot of chess. Dot Letski began writing a verse adaptation of *War and Peace*. The rest of us hacked around with the equipment, and making astronomical observations and gabbing. But all that began to get tiresome pretty fast, just as Kneffie said it would at the briefings. We talked about his idea that the best way to pass time in a spaceship was learning to get interested in mathematical problems—no mass to transport, no competitive element to get tempers up and all that. It began to make sense. So now Letski is in his tenth day of trying to find a formula for primes, and my own dear Flo is trying to prove Goldbach's Conjecture by means of the theory of congruences. (This is the girl who two months ago couldn't add up a laundry list!) It certainly passes the time.

Medically, we are all fit. I will append the detailed data on our blood pressures, pulses, etc., as well as the tape from the rocket and navigating systems readouts. I'll report again as scheduled. Take care of Earth for us—we're looking forward to seeing it again, in a few years!

Washington One

There was a lull in the urban guerrilla war in Washington that week. The chopper was able to float right in to the South Lawn of the White House—no sniper fire, no heat-seeking missiles, not even rock-throwing. Dr. Dieter von Knefhausen stared suspiciously at the knot of weary-looking pickets in their permitted fifty yards of space along the perimeter. They didn't look militant, probably Gay Lib or, who knew what, maybe nature-food or single-tax; at any rate no rocks came from them, only a little disorganized booing as the helicopter landed. Knefhausen bowed to Herr Omnes sardonically, hopped nimbly out of the chopper and got out of the way as it took off again, which it did at once. He didn't trouble to run to the White House. He strolled. He did not fear these simple people, even if the helicopter pilot did. Also he was not really eager to keep his appointment with the President.

The ADC who frisked him did not smile. The orderly who conducted him to the West Terrace did not salute. No one relieved him of the dispatch case with his slides and papers, although it was heavy. You could tell right away when you were in the doghouse,

5

he thought, ducking his head from the rotor blast as the pilot circled the White House to gain altitude before venturing back across the spread-out city.

It had been a lot different in the old days, he thought with some nostalgia. He could remember every minute of those old days. It was right here, this portico, where he had stood before the world's press and photographers to tell them about the Alpha-Aleph Project. He had seen his picture next to the President's on all the front-pages, watched himself on the TV newscasts, talking about the New Earth that would give America an entire colonizable planet four light-years away. He remembered the launch at the Cape, with a million and a half invited guests from all over the world: foreign statesmen and scientists eating their hearts out with envy, American leaders jovial with pride. The orderlies saluted then, all right. His lecture fees had gone clear out of sight. There was even talk of making him the Vice Presidential candidate in the next election—and it could have happened, too, if the election had been right then, and if there hadn't been the problem of his being born in another country.

Now it was all different. He was taken up in the service elevator. It wasn't so much that Knefhausen minded for his own sake, he told himself, but how did the word get out that there was trouble? Was it only the newspaper stories? Was there a leak?

The Marine orderly knocked once on the big door of the Cabinet room, and it was opened from inside.

Knefhausen entered.

No "Come in, Dieter, boy, pull up a pew." No Vice President jumping up to grab his arm and slap his back. His greeting was thirty silent faces turned toward him, some reserved, some frankly hostile. The full Cabinet was there, along with half a dozen department heads and the President's personal action staff, and the most hostile face around the big oval table was the President's own.

Knefhausen bowed. An atavistic hankering for lyceum-cadet jokes made him think of clicking his heels and adjusting a monocle, but he didn't have a monocle and didn't yield to impulses like that. He merely took his place standing at the foot of the table and, when the President nodded, said, "Good morning, gentlemen, and ladies. I assume you want to see me about the stupid lies the Russians are spreading about the Alpha-Aleph program."

Roobarooba, they muttered to each other. The President said in his sharp tenor, "So you think they are just lies?"

"Lies or mistakes, Mr. President, what's the difference? We are right and they are wrong, that's all."

Roobaroobarooba. The Secretary of State looked inquiringly at the President, got a nod and said: "Dr. Knefhausen, you know I've been on your team a long time and I don' want to disagree with any statement you care to make, but are you so sure about that? They's some mighty persuasive figures comin' out of the Russians."

"They are false, Mr. Secretary."

"Ah, well, Dr. Knefhausen. I might be inclined to take your word for it, but they's others might not. Not cranks or malcontents, Dr. Knefhausen, but good, decent people. Do you have any evidence for such as them?"

"With your permission, Mr. President?" The President nodded again, and Knefhausen unlocked his dispatch case and drew out a slim sheaf of slides. He handed them to a major of Marines, who looked to the President for approval and then did what Knefhausen told him. The room lights went down and, after some fiddling with the focus, the first slide was projected over Knefhausen's head. It showed a huge array of Y-shaped metal posts, stretching away into the distance of a bleak, powdery-looking landscape.

"This picture is our radio telescope on Farside, the Moon," he said. "It is never visible from the Earth, because that portion of the Moon's surface is permanently turned away from us, for which reason we selected it for the site of the telescope. There is no electrical interference of any kind. The instrument is made up of 33 million separate dipole elements, aligned with an accuracy of one part in several million. Its actual size is an approximate circle eighteen miles across, but by virtue of the careful positioning its performance is effectively equal to a telescope with a diameter of some twenty-six miles. Next slide, please."

Click. The picture of the huge RT display swept away and was replaced by another similar—but visibly smaller and shabbier—construction.

"This is the Russian instrument, gentlemen. And ladies. It is approximately one quarter the size of ours in diameter. It has less than one-tenth as many elements, and our reports—they are classified, but I am informed this gathering is cleared to receive this material? Yes—our reports indicate the alignment is very crude. Even terrible, you could say.

"The difference between the two instruments in information-gathering capacity is roughly a hundred to one, in our favor. Lights, please.

"What this means," he went on smoothly, smiling at each of the persons around the table in turn as he spoke, "is that if the Russians say 'no' and we say 'yes,' bet on 'yes.' Our radio telescope can be trusted. Theirs cannot."

The meeting shifted uneasily in its chairs. They were as anxious to believe Knefhausen as he was to convince them, but they were not sure.

Representative Belden, the Chairman of the House Ways and Means Committee, spoke for all of them. "Nobody doubts the quality of your equipment. Especially," he added, "since we still have bruises from the job of paying for it. But the Russians made a flat statement. They said that Alpha Centauri can't have a planet larger than one thousand miles in diameter, or nearer than half a billion miles to the star. I have a copy of the Tass release here. It admits that their equipment is inferior to our own, but they have a statement signed by twenty-two academicians that says their equipment could not miss on any object larger or nearer than what I have said, or on any body of any kind which would be large enough to afford a landing place for our astronauts. Are you familiar with this statement?"

"Yes, of course, I have read it—"

"Then you know that they state positively that the planet you call 'Alpha-Aleph' does not exist."

"Yes, that is what they state."

"Moreover, statements from authorities at the Paris Observatory and the UNESCO Astrophysical Center at Trieste, and from England's Astronomer Royal, all say that they have checked and confirmed their figures."

Knefhausen nodded cheerfully. "That is correct, Representative Belden. They confirm that if the observations are as stated, then the conclusions drawn by the Soviet installation at Novy Brezhnevgrad on Farside naturally follow. I don't question the arithmetic. I only say that the observations are made with inadequate equipment, and thus the Soviet astronomers have come to a false conclusion. But I do not want to burden your patience with an unsupported statement," he added hastily as the Congressman opened his mouth to speak again, "so I will tell you all there is to tell. What the Russians say is theory. What I have to counter is not merely better theory, but also objective

9

fact. I know Alpha-Aleph is there because I have seen it! Lights again, Major! And the next slide, if you please."

The screen lit up and showed glaring bare white with a sprinkling of black spots, like dust. A large one appeared in the exact center of the screen, with a dozen lesser ones sprinkled around it. Knefhausen picked up a flash pointer and aimed its little arrowhead of light at the central dot.

"This is a photographic negative," he said, "which is to say that it is black where the actual scene is white and vice versa. Those objects are astronomical. It was taken from our Briareus Twelve satellite near the orbit of Jupiter, on its way out to Neptune fourteen months ago. The central object is the star Alpha Centauri. It was photographed with a special instrument which filters out most of the light from the star itself, electronic in nature and something like the coronascope which is used for photographing prominences on our own Sun. We hoped that by this means we might be able actually to photograph the planet Alpha-Aleph. We were successful, as you can see." The flashpointer laid its little arrow next to the nearest small dot to the central star. "That, gentlemen, and ladies, is Alpha-Aleph. It is precisely where we predicted it from radio-telescope data."

There was another buzz from the table. In the dark it was louder than before. The Secretary of State cried sharply, "Mr. President! Can't we release this photograph?"

"We will release it immediately after this meeting," said the President.

Roobarooba. Then the committee chairman: "Mr. President, I'm sure if you say that's the planet we want, then it's the planet. But others outside this country may wonder, for indeed all those dots look about alike to me. I wonder if Knefhausen could satisfy a layman's curiosity. *How* do we know that's Alpha-Aleph?"

"Slide Number Four, please—and keep Number Three in the carriage." The same scene, subtly different. "Note that in this picture, gentlemen, that one object, there, is in a different position. It has moved. You know that the stars show no discernible motion, of course. It has moved because this photograph was taken eight months later, as Briareus Twelve was returning from the Neptune flyby, and the planet Alpha-Aleph had revolved in its orbit. This is not theory, it is evidence; and I add that the original tapes from which the photoprint was made are stored in Goldstone, so there is no question that arises of foolishness." *Roobarooba,* but in a higher and excited key. Gratified, Knefhausen nailed down his point. "So, Major, if you will now return to Slide Three, yes— And if you will flip back and forth, between Three and Four, as fast as you can— Thank you." The little black dot called Alpha-Aleph bounced back and forth like a tennis ball, while all the other star points remained motionless. "This is what is called the blink comparator process, you see. I point out that if what you are looking at is not a planet, it is, excuse me, Mr. President, the damnedest funniest star you ever saw. Also it is exactly at the distance and exactly with the orbital period we specified based on the RT data. Now, are there any more questions?"

"No, sir!" "That's great, Kneffie!" "Clear as a cow's ass to the stud bull." "I think that wraps it up." "That'll show the Commies."

The President's voice overrode them all.

"I think we can have the lights on now, Major Merton," he said. "Dr. Knefhausen, thank you. I'd appreciate it if you would remain nearby for a few minutes, so you can join Murray and myself in the

11

study to check over the text of our announcement before we release these pictures." He nodded sober dismissal to his chief science advisor and then, reminded by the happy faces of his cabinet, remembered to smile with pleasure.

Constitution Two

Sheffield Jackman's log. Starship *Constitution*. Day 95.

According to Letski we are now traveling at just about 15% of the speed of light, almost 30,000 miles per second. The fusion thrust is operating smoothly and well. Fuel, power, and life-support curves are sticking tight to optimum. No sweat of any kind with the ship, or, actually, with anything else.

Relativistic effects have begun to show up as predicted. Jim Barstow's spectral studies show the stars in front of us are showing a shift to the blue end, and the Sun and the other stars behind us are shifting to the red. Without the spectroscope you can't see much, though. Beta Circini looks a little funny, maybe. As for the Sun, it's still very bright—Jim logged it as minus-six magnitude a few hours ago—and as I've never seen it in quite that way before, I can't tell whether the color looks bright or not. It certainly isn't the golden yellow I associate with type G0, but neither is Alpha Centauri ahead of us, and I don't really see a difference between them. I think the reason is simply that they are so bright that the color impressions are secondary to the brightness impressions, although the spectroscope, as I say, does show the differences. We've all taken turns at looking back. Naturally enough, I guess. We can still make out the Earth and even the Moon in the telescope, but it's chancy. Ski almost got an eyeful of the Sun at full light-gathering amplitude yesterday because the visual separation is only about twelve seconds of arc now. In a few more days they'll be too close to separate.

Let's see, what else?

We've been having a fine time with the recreational-math program. Ann has taken to binary arithmetic like a duck to water. She's involved in what I take to be some sort of statistical experimentation (we don't pry too much into what the others are doing until they're ready to talk about it), and, of all things, she demanded we produce coins to flip. Well, naturally none of us had taken any money with us! Except that it turns out two of us did. Ski had a Russian silver ruble that his mother's uncle had given him for luck, and I found an old Philadelphia transit token in my pocket. Ann rejected my transit token as too light to be reliable, but she now spends happy hours flipping the ruble, heads or tails, and writing down the results as a series of six-place binary numbers, heads for 1 and tails for 0. After about a week my curiosity got too much so I began hinting to find out what she was doing. When I ask she says things like, "By means of the easy and the simple we grasp the laws of the whole world." When I say that's nice but what does she hope to grasp by flipping the coin? she says, "When the laws of the whole world are grasped, therein lies perfection." So, as I say, we don't press each other and I leave it there. But it passes the time.

Kneffie would be proud of himself if he could see how our recreation keeps us busy. None of us has managed to prove Fermat's Last Theorem yet or anything like that, but of course that's the whole point. If we could *solve* the problems, we'd have used them

13

up, and then what would we do for recreation? It does exactly what it was intended to. It keeps us mentally alert on this long and intrinsically rather dull boat-ride.

Personal relationships? Jes' fine, fellows, jes' fine. A lot better than any of us really hoped, back there at the personal-hygiene briefings in Mission Control. The girls take the stripey pills every day until three days before their periods, then they take the green pills for four days, then they lay off pills for four days, then back to the stripes. There was a little embarrassed joking about it at first, but now it's strictly routine, like brushing the teeth. We men take our red pills every day (Ski christened them "stop lights") until our girls tell us they're about to lay off (you know what I mean, each of our individual girls tells her husband), then we take the Blue Devil (that's what we call the antidote) and have a hell of a time until the girls start on the stripes again. None of us thought any of this would work, you know. But it works fine. I don't even think sex until Flo kisses my ear and tells me she's getting ready to, excuse the expression, get in heat, and then like wow. Same with everybody. The aft chamber with the nice wide bunks we call Honeymoon Hotel. It belongs to whoever needs it, and never once have both bunks been used. The rest of the time we just sleep wherever is convenient, and nobody gets uptight about it.

Excuse my getting personal, but you told me you wanted to know everything, and there's not much else to tell. All systems remain optimum. We check them over now and again, but nothing has given any trouble, or even looked as though it might be thinking about giving trouble later on. And there's absolutely nothing worth looking at outside but stars. We've all seen them about as much as we need to by now. The plasma jet thrums right along at our point-seven-five Gee. We don't even hear it any more.

We've even got used to the recycling system. None of us really thought we'd get with the suction toilet, not to mention what happens to the contents, but it was only a little annoying the first few days. Now it's fine. The treated product goes into the algae tanks, feces and urine together. The sludge from the algae goes into the hydroponic beds, but by then, of course, it's just greeny-brown vegetable matter like my father used to get out of his mulch bed. That's all handled semi-automatically anyway, of course, so our first real contact with the system comes in the kitchen. The food we eat comes in the form of nice red tomatoes and nourishing rice pilaff and stuff like that. (We do miss animal protein a little; the frozen stores have to last a long time, so each hamburger is a special feast, and we only have them once a week or so.) The water we drink comes actually out of the air, condensed by the dehumidifiers into the reserve supply, where we get it to drink. It's nicely aerated and chilled and tastes fine. Of course, the way it gets into the air in the first place is by being sweated out of our pores or transpired from the plants (which are irrigated direct from the treated product of the reclamation tanks), and we all know, when we stop to think of it, that every molecule of it has passed through all our kidneys forty times by now. But not directly. That's the point. What we drink is clear sweet dew. And if it once was something else, can't you say the same of Lake Erie?

Well. I think I've gone on long enough. You've probably got the idea by now: We're happy in the service, and we all thank you for giving us this pleasure cruise!

Washington Two

Waiting for his appointment with the President, Dr. Knefhausen re-read the communique from the spaceship, chuckling happily to himself. "Happy in the service." "Like wow." "Kneffie would be proud of himself"—indeed Kneffie was. And proud of them, those little wonders, there! So brave. So strong.

He took as much pride in them as if they had been his own sons and daughters, all eight of them. Everybody knew the Alpha-Aleph project was Knefhausen's baby, but he tried to conceal from the world that, in his own mind, he spread his fatherhood to include the crew. They were the pick of the available world, and it was he who had put them where they were. He lifted his head, listening to the distant chanting from the perimeter fence where today's disgusting exhibition of mob violence was doing its best to harass the people who were making the world go. What great lumps they were out there, with their long hair and their dirty morals. The heavens belonged only to angels, and it was Dieter von Knefhausen who had picked the angels. It was he who had established the selection procedures (and if he had done some things that were better left unmentioned to make sure the procedures worked, what of it?) It was he who had conceived and adapted the highly important recreation schedule, and above all he who had conceived the entire project and persuaded the President to make it come true. The hardware was nothing, only money. The basic scientific concepts were known; most of the components were on the shelves; it took only will to put them together. The will would

16

not have existed if it had not been for Knefhausen, who announced the discovery of Alpha-Aleph from his radio-observatory on Farside (and gave it that name, although as everyone realized he could have called it by any name he chose, even his own) and carried on the fight for the project by every means available until the President bought it.

It had been a hard, bitter struggle. He reminded himself with courage that the worst was still ahead. No matter. Whatever it cost, it was done, and it was worthwhile. These reports from *Constitution* proved it. It was going exactly as planned, and—

"Excuse me, Dr. Knefhausen."

He looked up, catapulted back from almost half a light-year away.

"I said the President will see you now, Dr. Knefhausen," repeated the usher.

"Ah," said Knefhausen. "Oh, yes, to be sure. I was deep in thought."

"Yes, sir. This way, sir."

They passed a window and there was a quick glimpse of the turmoil at the gates, picket signs used like battle-axes, a thin blue cloud of tear gas, the sounds of shouting. "King Mob is busy today," said Knefhausen absently.

"There's no danger, sir. Through here, please."

The President was in his private study, but to Knefhausen's surprise he was not alone. There was Murray Amos, his personal secretary, which one could understand; but there were three other men in the room. Knefhausen recognized them as the Secretary of State, the Speaker of the House and, of all people, the Vice President. How strange, thought Knefhausen, for what was to have been a confidential briefing for the President alone! But he rallied quickly.

"Excuse me, Mr. President," he said cheerfully. "I

17

must have understood wrong. I thought you were ready for our little talk."

"I am ready, Knefhausen," said the President. The cares of his years in the White House rested heavily on him today, Knefhausen thought critically. He looked very old and very tired. "You will tell these gentlemen what you would have told me."

"Ah, yes, I see," said Knefhausen, trying to conceal the fact that he did not see at all. Surely the President did not mean what his words said; therefore it was necessary to try to see what was his thought. "Yes, to be sure. Here is something, Mr. President. A new report from the *Constitution!* It was received by burst transmission from the Lunar Orbiter at Goldstone just an hour ago, and has just come from the decoding room. Let me read it to you. Our brave astronauts are getting along splendidly, just as we planned. They say—"

"Don't read us that just now," said the President harshly. "We'll hear it, but first there is something else. I want you to tell this group the full story of the Alpha-Aleph project."

"The full story, Mr. President?" Knefhausen hung on gamely. "I see. You wish me to begin with the very beginning, when first we realized at the observatory that we had located a planet—"

"No, Knefhausen. Not the cover story. The truth."

"Mr. President!" cried Knefhausen in sudden agony. "I must inform you that I protest this premature disclosure of vital—"

"The truth, Knefhausen!" shouted the President. It was the first time Knefhausen had ever heard him raise his voice. "It won't go out of this room, but you must tell them everything. Tell them why it is that the Russians were right and we lied! Tell them why we

18

sent the astronauts on a suicide mission, ordered to land on a planet that we knew all along did not exist!"

Constitution Three

Shef Jackman's journal, Day 130.

It's been a long time, hasn't it? I'm sorry for being such a lousy correspondent. I was in the middle of a thirteen-game chess series with Eve Barstow—she was playing the Bobby Fischer games, and I was playing in the style of Reshevsky—and Eve said something that made me think of old Kneffie, and that, of course, reminded me I owed you a transmission. So here it is.

In my own defense, though, it isn't only that we've been busy with other things. It takes a lot of power for these chatty little letters. Some of us aren't so sure they're worthwhile. The farther we get the more power we need to accumulate for a transmission. Right now it's not so bad yet, but, well, I might as well tell you the truth, right? Kneffie made us promise that. Always tell the truth, he said, because you're part of the experiment, and we need to know what you're doing, all of it. Well, the truth in this case is that we were a little short of disposable power for a while because Jim Barstow needed quite a lot for research purposes. You will probably wonder what the research is, but we have a rule that we don't criticize, or even talk about, what anyone else is doing until they're ready, and he isn't ready yet. I take the responsibility for the whole thing, not just the power drain but the damage to the ship. I said he could go ahead with it.

We're going pretty fast now, and to the naked eye

the stars fore and aft have blue-shifted and red-shifted nearly out of sight. It's funny, but we haven't been able to observe Alpha-Aleph yet, even with the disk obscuring the star. Now, with the shift to the blue, we probably won't see it at all until we slow down. We can still see the Sun, but I guess what we're seeing is ultraviolet when it's home. Of course the relativistic frequency shifts mean we need extra compensating power in our transmissions, which is another reason why, all in all, I don't think I'll be writing home every Sunday, between breakfast and the baseball game, the way I ought to!

But the mission's going along fine. The "personal relationships" keep on being just great. We've done a little experimental research there too that wasn't on the program, but it's all okay. No problems. Worked out great. I think maybe I'll leave out some of the details, but we found some groovy ways to do things. Oh, hell, I'll give you one hint: Dot Letski says I should tell you to get the boys at Mission Control to crack open two of the stripey pills and one of the Blue Devils, mix them with a quarter-teaspoon of black pepper and about 2 cc of the conditioner fluid from the recycling system. Serve over orange sherbet, and oh boy. After the first time we had it Flo made a crack about its being "seminal," which I thought was a private joke, but it broke everybody up. Dot figured it out for herself weeks ago. We wondered how she got so far so fast with *War and Peace* until she let us into the secret. Then we found out what it could do for you, both emotionally and intellectually: the creative over the arousing, as they say.

Ann and Jerry Letski used up their own recreational programs early (real early—they were supposed to last the whole voyage!), so they swapped microfiches, on the grounds that each was interested in an aspect

20

of causality and they wanted to see what the other side had to offer. Now Ann is deep into people like Kant and Carnap, and Ski is sore as a boil because there's no *Achillea millefolium* in the hydroponics garden. Needs the stalks for his researches, he says. He is making do with flipping his ruble to generate hexagrams; in fact, we all borrow it now and then, but it's not the right way. Honestly, Mission Control, he's right. Some thought should have been given to our other needs, besides sex and number theory. We can't even use chop bones from the kitchen wastes, because there isn't any kitchen waste. I know you couldn't think of everything, but still— Anyway, we improvise as best we can, and mostly well enough.

Let's see, what else? Did I send you Jim Barstow's proof of Goldbach's Conjecture? Turned out to be very simple once he had devised his multiplex parity analysis idea. Mostly we don't fool with that sort of stuff any more, though. We got tired of number theory after we'd worked out all the fun parts, and if there is any one thing that we all work on (apart from our private interests) it is probably the calculus of statement. We don't do it systematically, only as time permits from our other activities, but we're all pretty well convinced that a universal grammar is feasible enough, and it's easy enough to see what that leads to. Flo has done more than most of us. She asked me to put in that Boole, Venn and all those old people were on the wrong track, but she thinks there might be something to Leibniz's "calculus ratiocinator" idea. There's a J. W. Swanson suggestion that she likes for multiplexing languages. (Jim took off from it to work out his parity analysis.) The idea is that you devise a double-vocabulary language. One set of meanings is conveyed, say, by phonemes—that is, the shape of the words themselves. Another set is conveyed by pitch. It's like singing a message, half of it conveyed by the words, the other half by the tune. Like rock music. You get both sets of meanings at the same time. She's now working on third, fourth, and nth dimensions so as to convey many kinds of meanings at once, but it's not very fruitful so far (except for using sexual intercourse as one of the communications media). Most of the senses available are too limited to convey much. By the way, we checked out all the existing "artificial languages" as best we could—put Will Becklund under hypnotic regression to recapture the Esperanto he'd learned as a kid, for instance. But they were all blind alleys. Didn't even convey as much as standard English or French.

Medical readouts follow. We're all healthy. Eve Barstow gave us a medical check to make sure. Ann and Ski had little rough spots in a couple of molars so she filled them for the practice more than because they needed it. I don't mean practice in filling teeth; she wanted to try acupuncture instead of procaine. Worked fine.

We all have this writing-to-Daddy-and-Mommy-from-Camp-Tanglewood feeling and we'd like to send you some samples of our home handicrafts. The trouble is there's so much of it. Everybody has something he's personally pretty pleased with, like Barstow's proof of most of the classic math problems and my multi-media adaptation of *Sur le pont d'Avignon*. It's hard to decide what to send you with the limited power available, and we don't want to waste it with junk. So we took a vote and decided the best thing was Ann's verse retelling of *War and Peace*. It runs pretty long. I hope the power holds it. I'll transmit as much of it as I can. . . .

Washington Three

Spring was well advanced in Washington. Along the Potomac the cherry blossoms were beginning to bud, and Rock Creek Park was the pale green of new leaves. Even through the *whap, whap* of the helicopter rotor Knefhausen could hear an occasional rattle of small-arms fire from around Georgetown, and the Molotov cocktails and tear gas from the big Water Gate apartment development at the river's edge were steaming the sky with smoke and fumes. They never stopped, thought Knefhausen irritably. What was the good of trying to save people like this?

It was distracting. He found himself dividing his attention into three parts—the scarred, greening landscape below; the escort fireships that orbited around his own chopper; and the papers on his lap. All of them annoyed him. He couldn't keep his mind on any of them. What he liked least was the report from the *Constitution*. He had had to get expert help in translating what it was all about, and he didn't like the need, and even less liked the results. What had gone wrong? They were his kids, hand-picked. There had been no hint, for instance, of hippiness in any of them, at least not past the age of twenty, and only for Ann Becklund and Florence Jackman even then. How had they got into this *I Ching* foolishness, and this stupid business with the *Achillea millefolium,* better known as the common yarrow? What "experiments"? Who started the disgustingly antiscientific acupuncture thing? How dared they depart from their programmed power budget for "research pur-

23

poses," and what were the purposes? Above all, what was the "damage to the ship"?

He scribbled on a pad:

> With immediate effect, cut out the nonsense. I have the impression you are all acting like irresponsible children. You are letting down the ideals of our program.
>
> Knefhausen

After running the short distance from the chopper pad to the shelter of the guarded White House entrance, he gave the slip to a page from the Message Center for immediate encoding and transmission to the *Constitution* via Goldstone, Lunar Orbiter and Farside Base. All they needed was a reminder, he persuaded himself, then they would settle down. But he was still worried as he peered into a mirror, patted his hair down, smoothed his mustache with the tip of a finger and presented himself to the President's chief secretary.

This time they went down, not up. Knefhausen was going to the basement chamber that had been successively Franklin Roosevelt's swimming pool, the White House press lounge, a TV studio for taping jolly little two-shots of the President with congressmen and senators for the folks back home to see, and, now, the heavily armored bunker in which anyone trapped in the White House in the event of a successful attack from the city outside could hold out for several weeks, during which time the Fourth Armored would surely be able to retake the grounds from its bases in Maryland. It was not a comfortable room, but it was a safe one. Besides being armored against attack, it was as thoroughly soundproof, spyproof and leakproof as any chamber in the world, not excepting the Under-Kremlin or the Colorado NOROM base.

Knefhausen was admitted and seated, while the

24

President and a couple of others were in whispered conversation at one end of the room, and the several dozen other people present craned their necks to stare at Knefhausen.

After a moment the President raised his head. "All right," he said. He drank from a crystal goblet of water, looking wizened and weary, and disappointed at the way a boyhood dream had turned out: the Presidency wasn't what it had seemed to be from Muncie, Indiana. "We all know why we're here. The government of the United States has given out information which was untrue. It did so knowingly and wittingly, and we've been caught at it. Now we want you to know the background, and so Dr. Knefhausen is going to explain the Alpha-Aleph project. Go ahead, Knefhausen."

Knefhausen stood up and walked unhurryingly to the little lectern set up for him, off to one side of the President. He opened his papers on the lectern, studied them thoughtfully for a moment with his lips pursed, and said:

"As the President has said, the Alpha-Aleph project is a camouflage. A few of you learned this some months ago, and then you referred to it with other words. 'Fraud.' 'Fake.' Words like that. But if I may say it in French, it is not any of those words, it is a legitimate *ruse de guerre*. Not the *guerre* against our political enemies, or even against the dumb kids in the streets with their Molotov cocktails and bricks. I do not mean those wars, I mean the war against ignorance. For you see, there were certain sings—certain *things* we had to know for the sake of science and progress. Alpha-Aleph was designed to find them out for us.

"I will tell you the worst parts first," he said. "Number one, there is no such planet at Alpha-Aleph. The Russians were right. Number two, we knew this all along. Even the photographs we produced were fakes,

25

and in the long run the rest of the world will find this out and they will know of our *ruse de guerre*. I can only hope that they will not find out too soon, for if we are lucky and keep the secret for a while, then I hope we will be able to produce good results to justify what we have done. Number three, when the *Constitution* reaches Alpha Centauri there will be no place for them to land, no way to leave their spacecraft, no sources of raw materials which they might be able to use to make fuel to return, no nothing but the star and empty space. This fact has certain consequences. The *Constitution* was designed with enough hydrogen fuel capacity for a one-way flight, plus maneuvering reserve. There will not be enough for them to come back, and the source they had hoped to tap, namely the planet Alpha-Aleph, does not exist, so they will not come back. Consequently they will die there. Those are the bad things to which I must admit."

There was a sighing murmur from the audience. The President was frowning absently to himself. Knefhausen waithed patiently for the medicine to be swallowed, then went on.

"You ask, then, why have we done this thing? Condemning eight young people to their death? The answer is simple: knowledge. To put it with other words, we must have the basic scientific knowledge we need to protect the free world. You are all familiar, I si—I believe, with the known fact that basic scientific advances have been very few these past ten years and more. Much R&D. Much technology. Much applications. But in the years since Einstein, or better since Weizsäcker, very little basic.

"But without the new basic knowledge, the new technology must soon stop developing. It will run out of steam, you see.

"Now I must tell you a story. It is a true scientific

26

story, not a joke; I know you do not want jokes from me at this time. There was a man named de Bono, a Maltese, who wished to investigate the process of creative thinking. There is not very much known about this process, but he had an idea how he could find something out. So he prepared for an experiment a room that was stripped of all furniture, with two doors, one across from the other. You go into one door, you go through the room, you walk out the other. He put at the door that was the entrance some material—two flat boards, some ropes. And he got as his subjects some young children. Now he said to the children, 'Now, this is a game we will play. You must go through this room and out the other door, that is all. If you do that, you win. But there is one rule. You must not touch the floor with your feet or your knees or with any part of your body or your clothing. We had here a boy,' he said, 'who was very athletic and walked across on his hands, but he was disqualified. You must not do that. Now go, and whoever does it fastest will win some chocolates.'

"So he took away all of the children but the first one and, one by one, they tried. There were ten or fifteen of them, and each of them did the same thing. Some it took longer to figure out, some figured it out right away, but it always was the same trick: They sat down on the floor, they took the boards and the ropes, and they tied one board to each foot and they walked across the room like on skis. The fastest one thought of the trick right away and was across in a few seconds. The slowest took many minutes. But it was the same trick for all of them, and that was the first part of the experiment.

"Now this Maltese man, de Bono, performed the second part of the experiment. It was exactly like the first, with one difference. He did not give them two boards. He only gave them one board.

"And in the second part every child worked out the same trick, too, but it was of course a different trick. They tied the rope to the end of the single board and then they stood on it, and jumped up, tugging the rope to pull the board forward, hopping and tugging, moving a little bit at a time, and every one of them succeeded. But in the first experiment the average time to cross was maybe forty-five seconds. And in the second experiment the average time was maybe twenty seconds. With one board they did their job faster than with two.

"Perhaps now some of you see the point. Why did not any of the children in the first group think of this faster method of going across the room? It is simple. They looked at what they were given to use for materials and, they are like all of us, they wanted to use everything. But they did not need everything. They could do better with less, in a different way."

Knefhausen paused and looked around the room, savoring the moment. He had them now, he knew. It was just as it had been with the President himself, three years before. They were beginning to see the necessity of what had been done, and the pale, upturned faces were no longer as hostile, only perplexed and a little afraid.

He went on:

"So that is what Project Alpha-Aleph is about, gentlemen and ladies. We have selected eight of the most intelligent human beings we could find—healthy, young, very adventurous. Very creative. We played on them a nasty trick, to be sure. But we gave them an opportunity no one has ever had. The opportunity to *think*. To think for *ten years*. To think about basic questions. Out there they do not have the extra board to distract them. If they want to know something they cannot run

28

to the library and look it up, and find that somebody has said that what they were thinking could not work. They must think it out for themselves.

"So in order to make this possible we have practiced a deception on them, and it will cost them their lives. All right, that is tragic, yes. But if we take their lives we give them in exchange immortality.

"How do we do this? Trickery again, gentlemen and ladies. I do not say to them, 'Here, you must discover new basic approaches to science and tell them to us.' I camouflage the purpose, so that they will not be distracted even by that. We have told them that this is recreational, to help them pass the time. This too is a ruse de guerre. The 'recreation' is not to help them make the trip; it is the whole purpose of the trip.

"So we start them out with the basic tools of science. With numbers: that is, with magnitudes and quantification, with all that scientific observations are about. With grammar. This is not what you learned when you were thirteen years old, it is a technical term; it means with the calculus of statement and the basic rules of communication: that is so they can learn to think clearly by communicating fully and without fuzzy ambiguity. We give them very little else, only the opportunity to mix these two basic ingredients and come up with new forms of knowledge.

"What will come of these things? That is a fair question. Unfortunately there is no answer. Not yet. If we knew the answer in advance, we would not have to perform the experiment. So we do not know what will be the end result of this, but already they have accomplished very much. Old questions that have puzzled the wisest of scientists for hundreds of years they have solved already. I will give you one example. You will say, 'yes, but what does it *mean?*' I will answer, 'I do not know'; I only know that it is so hard a question that no one else has ever been able to answer it. It is a proof of a thing which is called Goldbach's Conjecture. Only a conjecture; you could call it a guess. A guess by an eminent mathematician some many years ago, that every even number can be written as the sum of two prime numbers. This is one of those simple problems in mathematics that everyone can understand and no one can solve. You can say, 'Certainly, sixteen is the sum of eleven and five, both of which are prime numbers, and thirty is the sum of twenty-three and seven, which also are both prime, and I can give you such numbers for any even number you care to name.' Yes, you can; but can you prove that for *every* even number it will *always* be possible to do this? No. You cannot. No one has been able to, but our friends on the *Constitution* have done it, and this was in the first few months. They have yet almost ten years. I cannot say what they will do in that time, but it is foolish to imagine that it will be anything less than very much indeed. A new relativity, a new universal gravitation—I don't know, I am only saying words. But much."

He paused again. No one was making a sound. Even the President was no longer staring straight ahead without expression, but was looking at him.

"It is not yet too late to spoil the experiment, and so it is necessary for us to keep the secret a bit longer. But there you have it, gentlemen and ladies. That is the truth about Alpha-Aleph." He dreaded what would come next, postponed it for a second by consulting his papers, shrugged, faced them and said: "Now, are there any questions?"

Oh, yes there were questions. *Herr Omnes* was stunned a little, took a moment to overcome the spell of the simple and beautiful truths he had heard, but then first one piped up, then another, then two or three shouting at once. There were questions, to be sure. Questions beyond answering. Questions Knefhausen did not have time to hear, much less answer, before the next question was on him. Questions to which he did not know the answers. Questions, worst of all, to which the answers were like pepper in the eyes, enraging, blinding the people to sense. But he had to face them, and he tried to answer them. Even when they shouted so that, outside the thick double doors, the Marine guards looked at each other uneasily and wondered what made the dull rumble that penetrated the very good soundproofing of the room. "What I want to know, who put you up to this?" "Mr. Chairman, nobody; it is as I have said." "But see now, Knefhausen, do you mean to tell us you're murderin' these good people for the sake of some Goldbach's theory?" "No, Senator, not for Goldbach's Conjecture, but for what great advances in science will mean in the struggle to keep the free world free." "You're confessing you've dragged the United States into a palpable fraud?" "A legitimate ruse of war, Mr. Secretary, because there was no other way." "The photographs, Knefhausen?" "Faked, General, as I have told you. I accept full responsibility." And on and on, the words "murder" and "fraud" and even "treason" coming faster and faster.

Until at last the President stood up and raised his hand. Order was a long time coming, but at last they quieted down.

"Whether we like it or not, we're in it," he said simply. "There is nothing else to say. You have come to me, many of you, with rumors and asked for the truth. Now you have the truth, and it is classified Top Secret and must not be divulged. You all know what this means. I will only add that I personally propose to see that any breach of this security is investigated with

31

all the resources of the government, and punished with the full penalty of the law. I declare this a matter of national emergency, and remind you that the penalty includes the death sentence when appropriate—and I say that in this case it is appropriate." He looked very much older than his years, and he moved his lips as though something tasted bad in his mouth. He allowed no further discussion, and dismissed the meeting.

Half an hour later, in his private office, it was just Knefhausen and the President.

"All right," said the President, "it's all hit the fan. The next thing is: The world will know it. I can postpone that a few weeks, maybe even months. I can't prevent it."

"I am grateful to you, Mr. President, for—"

"Shut up, Knefhausen. I don't want any speeches. There is one thing I want from you, and that is an explanation. What the hell is this about mixing up narcotics and free love and so on?"

"Ah," said Knefhausen, "you refer to the most recent communication from the *Constitution*. Yes. I have already dispatched, Mr. President, a strongly worded order. Because of the communications lag it will not be received for some months, but I assure you the matter will be corrected."

The President said bitterly, "I don't want any assurances, either. Do you watch television? I don't mean *I Love Lucy* and ball games, I mean news. Do you know what sort of shape this county is in? The bonus marches in 1932, the race riots in 1967—they were nothing. Time was when we could call out the National Guard to put down disorder. Last week I had to call out the Army to use against three companies of the Guard. One more scandal and we're finished, Knefhausen, and this is a big one."

"The purposes are beyond reproach—"

"Your purposes may be. Mine may be, or I try to tell myself it is for the good of science I did this, and not so I will be in the history books as the president who contributed a major breakthrough. But what are the purposes of your friends on the *Constitution?* I agreed to eight martyrs, Knefhausen. I didn't agree to forty billion dollars out of the nation's pockets to give your eight young friends ten years of gang-bangs and dope."

"Mr. President, I assure you this is only a temporary phase. I have instructed them to straighten out."

"And if they don't, what are you going to do about it?" The President, who never smoked, stripped a cigar, bit off the end and lit it. He said, "It's too late for me to say I shouldn't have let you talk me into this. So all I will say is you have to show results from this flimflam before the lid blows off, or I won't be President any more, and I doubt that you will be alive."

Constitution Four

This is Shef again and it's, oh, let me see, about Day 250. 300? No, I don't think so. Look, I'm sorry about the ship date, but I honestly don't think much in those terms any more. I've been thinking about other things. Also I'm a little upset. When I tossed the ruble the hexagram was K'an, which is danger, over Li, the Sun. That's a bad mood to be communicating with you in. We aren't vengeful types, but the fact is that some of us were pretty sore when we found out what you'd done. I don't *think* you need to worry, but I wish I'd got a better hexagram.

Let me tell you the good parts first. Our velocity is

pushing point four oh C now. The scenery is beginning to get interesting. For several weeks now the stars fore and aft have been drifting out of sight as the ones in front get up into the ultraviolet and the ones behind sink into the infrared. You'd think that as the spectrum shifts the other parts of the EMF bands would come into the visible range. I guess they do, but stars peak in certain frequencies, and most of them seem to do it in the visible frequencies, so the effect is that they disappear. The first thing was that there was a sort of round black spot ahead of us where we couldn't see anything at all, not Alpha Centauri, not Beta Centauri, not even the bright Circini stars. Then we lost the Sun behind us, and a little later we saw the blackout spread to a growing circle of stars there. Then the circles began to widen.

Of course, we know that the stars are really there. We can detect them with phase-shift equipment, just as we can transmit and receive your messages by shifting the frequencies. But we just can't see them any more. The ones in direct line of flight, where we have a vector velocity of .34c or .37c (depending on whether they are in front of us or behind us) simply aren't radiating in the visible band any more. The ones farther out to the side have been displaced visually because of the relativistic effects of our speed. But what it looks like is that we're running the hell out of Nothing, in the direction of Nothing, and it is frankly a little scary.

Even the stars off to one side are showing relativistic color shifts. It's almost like a rainbow, one of those full-circle rainbows that you see on the clouds beneath you from an airplane sometimes. Only this circle is all around us. Nearest the black hole in front the stars have frequency-shifted to a dull reddish color. They go through orange and yellow and a sort of leaf green to the band nearest the back hole in back, which are bright blue shading to purple. Jim Barstow has been practicing his farsight on them, and he can relate them to the actual sky map. But I can't. He sees something in the black hole in front of us that I can't see, either. He says he thinks it's a bright radio source, probably Centaurus A, and he claims it is radiating strongly in the whole visible band now. He means strongly for him, with his eyes. I'm not sure I can see it at all. There *may* be a sort of very faint, diffuse glow there, like the *gegenschein,* but I'm not sure. Neither is anyone else.

But the starbow itself is beautiful. It's worth the trip. Flo has been learning oil painting so she can make a picture of it to send you for your wall, although when she found out what you'd been up to she got so sore she was thinking of boobytrapping it with a fusion bomb or something. (But she's over that now. I think.)

So we're not so mad at you any more, although there was a time when, if I'd been communicating with you at exactly that moment, I would have said some bad things.

. . . . I just played this back, and it sounds pretty jumbled and confused. I'm sorry about that. It's hard for me to do this. I don't mean hard like intellectually difficult (the way chess problems and tensor analysis used to be), but hard like shoveling sand with a tea-spoon. I'm just not used to constricting my thoughts in this straitjacket any more. I tried to get one of the others to communicate this time instead of me, but there were no takers. I did get a lot of free advice. Dot says I shouldn't waste my time remembering how we used to talk. She wanted to write an eidetic account in simplified notation for you, which she estimated a crash program could translate for you in reasonable time, a decade or two, and would give you an absolutely full account of everything. I objected that that involved practical difficulties. Not in preparing the account, I don't mean. Shucks, we can all do that now. I don't forget anything, except irrelevant things like the standard-reckoning day that I don't want to remember in the first place, and neither does anyone else. But the length of transmission would be too much. We don't have the power to transmit the necessary number of groups, especially since the accident. Dot said we could Gödelize it. I said you were too dumb to de-Gödelize it. She said it would be good practice for you.

Well, she's right about that, and it's time you all learned how to communicate in a sensible way, so if the power holds out I'll include Dot's eidetic account at the end. In Gödelized form. Lots of luck. I won't honestly be surprised if you miss a digit or something and it all turns into *Rebecca of Sunnybrook Farm* or some missing books of apocrypha or, more likely of course, gibberish. Ski says it won't do you any good in any case, because Henle was right. I pass that on without comment.

Sex. You always want to hear about sex. It's great. Now that we don't have to fool with the pills any more we've been having some marvelous times. Flo and Jim Barstow began making it as part of a multiplexed communications system that you have to see to believe. Sometimes when they're going to do it we all knock off and just sit around and watch them, cracking jokes and singing and helping with the auxiliary computations. When we had that little bit of minor surgery the other day (now we've got the bones seasoning), Ann and Ski decided to ball instead of using anesthesia, and they said it was better than acupuncture. It didn't block the sensation. They were aware of their little toes being lopped off, but they didn't perceive it as pain. So then Jim, when it was his turn, tried going through the amputation without anything at all in the expectation that he and Flo would go to bed together a little later, and that worked well too. He was all het up about it;

claimed it showed a reverse causality that his theories predicted but that had not been demonstrated before. Said at last he was over the cause-preceding-the-effect hangup. It's like the Red Queen and the White Queen, and quite puzzling until you get the hang of it. (I'm not sure I've gotten the hang of it yet.) Supposed he hadn't balled Flo? Would his toe have hurt retroactively? I'm a little mixed up on this, Dot says because I simply don't understand phenomenology in general, and I think I'll have to take Ann's advice and work my way through Carnap, although the linguistics are so poor that it's hard to stay with it. Come to think of it, I don't have to. It's all in the Gödelized eidetic statement, after all. So I'll transmit the statement to you, and while I'm doing that it will be a sort of review for me and maybe I'll get my head right on causality.

Listen, let me give you a trip. The statement will also include Ski's trick of containing plasma for up to 500K milliseconds, so when you figure it out you'll know how to build those fusion power reactors you were talking about when we left. That's the carrot before your nose, so get busy on de-Gödelizing. The plasma dodge works fine, although of course we were sorry about what happened when we converted the drive. The explosion killed Will Becklund outright, and it looked hairy for all of us.

Well, anyway. I have to cut this short because the power's running a little low and I don't want to chance messing up the statement. It follows herewith:

$$1973^{354} + 331^{852} + 17^{2008} + 5^{47} + 3^{9606} + 2^{88}$$

take away 78.

Lots of luck, fellows!

Washington Four

Knefhausen lifted his head from the litter of papers on his desk. He rubbed his eyes, sighing. He had given up smoking the same time as the President, but, like the President, he was thinking of taking it up again. It could kill you, yes. But it was a tension-reducer, and he needed that. And what was wrong with something killing you. There were worse things than being killed, he thought dismally.

Looking at it any way you could, he thought objectively, the past two or three years had been hard on him. They had started so well and had gone so bad. Not as bad as those distant memories of childhood when everybody was so poor and Berlin was so cold and what warm clothes he had came from the *Winterhilfe*. By no means as hard as the end of the war. Nothing like as bad as those first years in South America and then in the Middle East, when even the lucky and famous ones, the Von Brauns and the Ehrickes, were having trouble getting what was due them and a young calf like Knefhausen had to peel potatoes and run elevators to live. But harder and worse than a man at the summit of his career had any reason to expect.

The Alpha-Aleph project, fundamentally, was sound! He ground his teeth, thinking about it. It would work —no, by God, it *was* working, and it would make the world a different place. Future generations would see.

But the future generations were not here yet, and in the present things were going badly.

Reminded, he picked up the phone and buzzed his

secretary. "Have you got through to the President yet?" he demanded.

"I'm sorry, Dr. Knefhausen. I've tried every ten minutes, just as you said."

"Ah," he grunted. "No, wait. Let me see. What calls are there?"

Rustle of paper. "The news services, of course, asking about the rumors again. Jack Anderson's office. The man from CBS."

"No, no. I will not talk to press. Anyone else?"

"Senator Copley called, asking when you were going to answer the list of questions his committee sent you."

"I will give him an answer. I will give him the answer Götz von Berlichingen gave to the Bishop of Bamberg."

"I'm sorry, Dr. Knefhausen, I didn't quite catch—"

"No matter. Anything else?"

"Just a long-distance call, from a Mr. Hauptmann. I have his number."

"Hauptmann?" The name was puzzlingly familiar. After a moment Knefhausen placed it: to be sure, the photo technician who had cooperated in the faked pictures from Briareus Twelve. Well, he had his orders to stay out of sight and shut up. "No, that's not important. None of them are, and I do not wish to be disturbed with such nonsense. Continue as you were, Mrs. Ambrose. If the President is reached you are to put me on at once, but no other calls."

He hung up and returned to his desk.

He looked sadly and fondly at the papers. He had them all out: the reports from the *Constitution*, his own drafts of interpretation and comment, and more than a hundred footnoted items compiled by his staff, to help untangle the meanings and implications of those, ah, so cryptic sometimes reports from space:

"Henle. Apparently refers to Paul Henle (note appended); probably the citation intended is his statement, 'There are certain symbolisms in which certain things cannot be said.' Conjecture that English language is one of those symbolisms."

"Orange sherbet sundae. A classified experimental study was made of the material in Document Ref. No. CON-130, Para. 4. Chemical analysis and experimental testing have indicated that the recommended mixture of pharmaceuticals and other ingredients produce a hallucinogen-related substance of considerable strength and not wholly known qualities. 100 subjects ingested the product or a placebo in a double-blind controlled test. Subjects receiving the actual substance report reactions significantly different from the placebo. Effects reported include feelings of immense competence and deepened understanding. However, data is entirely subjective. Attempts were made to verify claims by standard I.Q., manipulative, and other tests, but the subjects did not cooperate well, and several have since absented themselves without leave from the testing establishment."

"Gödelized language. A system of encoding any message of any kind as a single very large number. The message is first written out in clear language and then encoded as bases and exponents. Each letter of the message is represented in order by the natural order of primes—that is, the first letter is represented by the base 2, the second by the base 3, the third by the base 5, then 7, 11, 13, 17, etc. The identity of the letter occupying that position in the message is given by the exponent: simply, the exponent 1 meaning that the letter in that position is an A, the exponent 2 meaning that it is a B, 3 a C, etc. The message as a whole is then rendered as the product of all the bases and exponents. *Example.* The word "cab" can thus be represented as 2^3 x 3^1 x 5^2, or 600. ($=8$x3x25.) The name 'Abe' would be represented by the number 56,250, or 2^1 x 3^2 x 5^5. ($=2$x9x3125.)

A sentence like 'John lives.' would be represented by the product of the following terms: 2^{10} x 3^{15} x 5^8 x 7^{14} x 11^0 x 13^{12} x 17^9 x 19^{22} x 23^5 x 29^{19} x 31^{27} (in which the exponent '0' has been reserved for a space and the exponent '27' has been arbitrarily assigned to indicate a full stop). As can be seen, the Gödelized form for even a short message involves a very large number, although such numbers may be transmitted quite compactly in the form of a sum of bases and exponents. The example transmitted by the *Constitution* is estimated to equal the contents of a standard unabridged dictionary."

"*Farsight.* The subject James Madison Barstow is known to have suffered from some nearsightedness in his early school years, apparently brought on by excessive reading, which he attempted to cure through eye exercises similar to the 'Bates method' (note appended). His vision at time of testing for Alpha-Aleph project was optimal. Interviews with former associates indicate his continuing interest in increasing visual acuity. *Alternate explanation.* There is some indication that he was also interested in paranormal phenomena such as clairvoyance or prevision, and it is possible, though at present deemed unlikely, that his use of the term refers to 'looking ahead' in time."

And so on, and on.

Knefhausen gazed at the litter of papers lovingly and hopelessly, and passed his hand over his forehead. The kids! They were so marvelous . . . but so unruly . . . and so hard to understand. How unruly of them to have concealed their true accomplishments. The secret of hydrogen fusion! That alone would justify, more than justify, the entire project. But where was it? Locked in that number-jumber gibberish. Knefhausen was not without appreciation of the elegance of the method. He, too, was capable of taking seriously a device of such luminous simplicity. Once the number was written out you had only to start by dividing it by two as many times as possible, and the number of times would give you the first letter. Then divide by the next prime, three, and that number of times would give you the second letter. But the practical difficulties! You could not get even the first letter until you had the whole number, and IBM had refused even to bid on constructing a bank of computers to write that number out unless the development time was stretched to twenty-five years. *Twenty-five years.* And meanwhile in that number was hidden probably the secret of hydrogen fusion, possibly many greater secrets, most certainly the key to Knefhausen's own well-being over the next few weeks. . . .

His phone rang.

He grabbed it and shouted into it at once: "Yes, Mr. President!"

He had been too quick. It was only his secretary. Her voice was shaking but determined.

"It's not the President, Dr. Knefhausen, but Senator Copley is on the wire and he says it is urgent. He says—"

"No!" shouted Knefhausen and banged down the phone. He regretted it even as he was doing it. Copley was very high, chairman of the Armed Forces Committee; he was not a man Knefhausen wished to have as an enemy, and he had been very careful to make him a friend over years of patient fence-building. But he could not speak to him, or to anyone, while the President was not answering his calls. Copley's rank was high, but he was not in the direct heirarchical line over Knefhausen. When the top of that line refused to talk to him, Knefhausen was cut off from the world.

He attempted to calm himself by examining the situation objectively. The pressures on the President just now: They were enormous. There was the continuing trouble in the cities, all the cities. There were the political conventions coming up. There was the need to get elected for a third term, and the need to get the law amended to make that possible. And yes, Knefhausen admitted to himself, the worst pressure of all was the rumors that were floating around about the *Constitution*. He had warned the President. It was unfortunate the President had not listened. He had said that a secret known to two people is compromised and a secret known to more than two is no secret. But the President had insisted on the disclosure to that ever-widening circle of high officials—sworn, of course to secrecy, but what good was that?—and, of course, in spite of everything, there had been leaks. Fewer than one might have feared. More than one could stand.

He touched the reports from *Constitution* caressingly. Those beautiful kids, they could still make everything right, so wonderful. . . .

Because it was he who had made them wonderful, he confessed to himself. He had invented the idea. He had selected them. He had done things which he did not quite even yet reconcile himself to to make sure that it was they and not some others who were on the crew. He had, above all, made assurance doubly sure by insuring their loyalty in every way possible. Training. Discipline. Ties of affection and friendship. More reliable ties: loading their food supplies, their entertainment tapes, their programmed activities with every sort of advertising inducement, M/R compulsion, psychological reinforcement he could invent or find, so that whatever else they did they did not fail to report faithfully back to Earth. Whatever else happened, there was that. The data might be hard to untangle, but it would be there. They could not help themselves; his commandments were stronegr than God's; like Martin Luther, they must say *Ich kann night anders,* and come Pope or inquisition, they must stand by it. They would learn, and tell what they learned, and thus the investment would be repaid. . . .

The telephone!

He was talking before he had it even to his mouth. "Yes, yes! This is Dr. Knefhausen, yes!" he gabbled. Surely it must be the President now—

It was not.

"Knefhausen!" shouted the man on the other end. "Now, listen, I'll tell you what I told that bitch pig girl of yours, if I don't talk to you on the phone *right now* I'll have Fourth Armored in there to arrest you and bring you to me in twenty minutes. So listen!"

Knefhausen recognized both voice and style. He drew a deep voice and forced himself to be calm. "Very well, Senator Copley," he said, "what is it?"

"The game is blown, boy! That's what it is. That boy of yours in Huntsville, what's his name, the photo technician—"

"Hauptmann?"

"That's him! Would you like to know where he is, you dumb Kraut bastard?"

"Why, I suppose—I should think in Huntsville—"

"Wrong, boy! Your Kraut bastard friend claimed he didn't feel good and took some accrued sick time. Intelligence kept an eye on him up to a point, didn't stop him, wanted to see what he'd do. Well, they saw. They saw him leaving Orly Airport an hour ago in an Aeroflot plane. Put your big Kraut brain to work on that one, Knefhausen! He's defected. Now start figuring out what you're going to do about it, and it better be good?"

Knefhausen said something, he did not know what, and hung up the phone, he did not remember when. He stared glassily into space for a time.

Then he flicked the switch for his secretary and said, not listening to her stammering apologies, "That long-distance call that came from Hauptmann before, Mrs. Ambrose. You didn't say where it was from."

"It was an overseas call, Dr. Knefhausen. From Paris. You didn't give me a chance to—"

"Yes, yes. I understand. Thank you. Never mind." He hung up and sat back. He felt almost relieved. If Hauptmann had gone to Russia it could only be to tell them that the picture was faked and not only was there no planet for the astronauts to land on but it was not a mistake, even, actually a total fraud. So now it was all out of his hands. History would judge him now. The die was cast. The Rubicon was crossed.

So many literary allusions, he thought deprecatingly. Actually it was not the judgment of history that was immediately important but the judgment of certain real people now alive and likely to respond badly. And they would judge him not so much by what might be or what should have been, as by what was. He shivered in the cold of that judgment and reached for the telephone to try once more to call the President. But he was quite sure the President would not answer, then or ever again.

Constitution Five

Old reliable peed-off Shef here. Look, we got your message. I don't want to discuss it. You've got a nerve. You're in a bad mood, aren't you? If you can't say anything nice, don't say anything at all. We do the best we can, and that's not bad, and if we don't do exactly what you want us to, maybe it's because we know quite a lot more than you did when you fired us off at that blob of moonshine you call Alpha-Aleph. Well, thanks a lot for nothing.

On the other hand, thanks a little for what little you did do, which at least worked out to get us where we are, and I don't mean spatially. So I'm not going to yell at you. I just don't want to talk to you at all. I'll let the other talk for themselves.

Dot Letski speaking. This is important. Pass it on. I have three things to tell you that I do not want you to forget. *One: Most problems have grammatical solutions.* The problem of transporting people from the Earth to another planet does not get solved by putting pieces of steel together one at a time at random, and happening to find out you've built the *Constitution* by accident. It gets solved by constructing a model (=equation (=grammar)) which describes the necessary circumstances under which the transportation occurs. Once you have the grammatical model, you just put the metal around it and it goes like gangbusters.

When you have understood this you will be ready for: *Two: There is no such thing as causality.* What a waste of time it has been, trying to assign "causes" to "events"! You say things like, "Striking a match causes it to burn." True statement? No, false statement. You find yourself in a whole waffle about whether the "act" of "striking" is "necessary" and/or "sufficient" and you get lost in words. Pragmatically useful grammars are without tenses. In a decent grammar (which this English-language one, of course, is not, but I'll do the best I can) you can make a statement like "There exists a conjunction of forms of matter (specified) which combine with the release of energy at a certain temperature (specified) (which may be the temperature associated with heat of friction)." Where's the causality? "Cause" and "effect" are in the same timeless statement. So, *Three: There are no such things as empirical laws.* When Ski came to understand that, he was able

46

to contain the plasma in our jet indefinitely, not by pushing particles around in brute-force magnetic squeezes but by encouraging them to want to stay together. There are other ways of saying what he does (="creates an environment in which centripetal exceed centrifugal forces"), but the way I said it is better because it tells something about your characters. Bullies, all of you. Why can't you be nice to things if you want them to be nice to you? Be sure to pass this on to T'in Fa at Tiantsin, Professor Morris at All Soul's, and whoever holds the Carnap chair at UCLA.

Flo's turn. My mother would have loved my garden. I have drumsticks and daffodils growing side by side in the sludgy sand. They do so please us, and we them: I will probably transmit a full horticultural handbook at a future date, but meanwhile it is shameful to eat a radish. Carrots, on the other hand, enjoy it.

A statement of William Becklund, decreased. I emerged into the world between feces and urine, learned, grew, ate, worked, moved and died. Alternatively, I emerged from the hydrogen flare, shrank, disgorged, and reentered the womb one misses so. You may approach it from either end, it makes no difference at all which way you look at it.

Observational datum, Letski. At time *t*, a Dirac number incommensurable with GMT, the following phenomenon is observed:

The radio source Centaurus A is identified as a positionally stable single collective object rather than two intersecting gas clouds and is observed to contract radially toward a center. Analysis and observation reveal it to be a Black Hole of which the fine detail is not detectable as yet. One infers all galaxies develop such central vortices, with implications of interest to astronomers and eschatologists. I, Seymour Letski, propose to take a closer look but the others prefer to continue programmed flight first. Harvard-Smithsonian notification service, please copy.

"Starbow", a preliminary study for a rendering into English of a poem by James Barstow:

> Gaggle of goslings but pick of our race
> We waddle through relativistic space.
> Dilated, discounted, despondent we scan:
> But vacant the Sign of the Horse and the Man.
> Vacant the Sign of the Man and the Horse,
> And now we conjecture the goal of our course.
> Tricked, trapped and cozened, we ruefully run
> After the child of the bachelor sun.
> The trick is revealed and the trap is confessed
> And we are the butts of the dimwitted jest.
> O Gander who made us, O Goose who laid us,
> How lewdly and twistedly you betrayed us!
> We owe you a debt. We won't foregt.
> With fortune and firmness we'll pay you yet.
> Give us some luck and we'll timely send
> Your pot of gold from the starbow's end.

Ann Becklund:

I think it was Stanley Weinbaum who said that from three facts a truly superior mind should be able to deduce the whole universe (Ski thinks it is possible with a finite number, but considerably larger than that). We are so very far from being truly superior minds by those standards, or even by our own. Yet we have a much larger number of facts to work with than three, or even three thousand, and so we have deduced a good deal.

This is not as valuable to you as you might have

48

hoped, dear old bastardly Kneffie and all you bastardly others, because one of the things that we have
deduced is that we can't tell you everything, because
you wouldn't understand. We would help you along,
some of you, if you were here, and in time you would
be able to do what we do easily enough, but not at
remote control.

But all is not lost, folks! Cheer up! You don't deduce
like we deduce, but on the other hand you have so
very much more to work from. Try. Get smart. You
can do it if you want to. Set your person at rest,
compose your mind before you speak, make your rela-
tions firm before you ask for something. Try not to
be loathsome about it. Don't be like the fellow in the
Changes. "He brings increase to no one. Indeed, someone even strikes him."

We've all grown our toes back now, even Will, although it was particularly difficult for him since he had
been killed, and we've inscribed the bones and used
them with very good effect in generating the hexagrams.
I hope you see the point of what we did. We could have
gone on with tossing coins or throwing the yarrow
stalks, or at least with the closest Flo could breed to
yarrow stalks. We didn't want to do that because it's
not the optimum way.

The person who doesn't keep his heart constantly
steady might say, "Well, what's the difference?" That's
a poor sort of question to ask. If implies a deterministic
answer. A better question is, "Does it make a difference?" and the answer to that is, "Yes, probably, because in order to do something right you must do it
right." That is the law of identity, in any language.

Another question you might ask is, "Well, what
source of knowledge are you actually tapping when you
consult the hexagrams?" That's a better kind of question in that it doesn't *force* a wrong answer, but the

answer is, again, indeterminate. You might view the *I Ching* as a sort of Rorschach bundle of squiggles that has no innate meaning but is useful because your own mind interprets it and puts sense into it. Feel free! You might think of it as a sort of memory bank of encoded lore. Why not? You might skip it entirely and come to knowledge in some other tao, any tao you like. ("The superior man understands the transitory in the light of the eternity of the end.") That's fine, too!

But whatever way you do it, you should *do* it that way. We needed inscribed bones to generate hexagrams, because that was the right way, and so it was no particular sacrifice to lop off a toe each for the purpose. It's working out nicely, except for one thing. The big hangup now is that the translations are so degraded, Chinese to German, German to English, and error seeping in at every step, but we're working on that now.

Perhaps I will tell you more at another time. Not now. Not very soon. Eve will tell you about that.

Eve Barstow, the Dummy, comes last and, I'm afraid, least.

When I was a little girl I used to play chess, badly, with very good players, and that's the story of my life. I'm a chronic over-achiever. I can't stand people who aren't smarter and better than I am, but the result is that I'm the runt of the litter every time. They are all very nice to me here, even Jim, but they know what the score is and so do I.

So I keep busy and applaud what I can't do. It isn't a bad life. I have everything I need, except pride.

Let me tell you what a typical day is like here between Sol and Centaurus. We wake up (if we have been sleeping, which some of us still do) and eat (if we are still eating, as all but Ski and, of course, Will

50

Becklund do). The food is delicious and Florence has induced it to grow cooked and seasoned where that is desirable, so it's no trouble to go over and pick yourself a nice poached egg or clutch of French fries. (I really prefer brioche in the mornings, but for sentimental reasons she can't manage them.) Sometimes we ball a little or sing old campfire songs. Ski comes down for that, but not for long, and then he goes back to looking at the universe. The starbow is magnificent and appalling. It is now a band about 40° across, completely surrounding us with colored light. One can always look in the other frequencies and see ghost stars before us and behind us, but in the birthright bands the view to the front and rear is now dead black and the only light is that beautiful banded ring of powdery stars.

Sometimes we write plays or have a little music. Shef had deduced four lost Bach piano concerti, very reminiscent of Corelli and Vivaldi, with everything going at once in the tuttis, and we've all adapted them for performance. I did mine on the Moog, but Ann and Shef synthesized whole orchestras. Shef's is particularly cute. You can tell that the flautist has early emphysema and two people in the violin section have been drinking, and he's got Toscanini conducting like a *risorgimento* metronome. Flo's oldest daughter made up words and now she sings a sort of nursery-rhyme adaptation of some Buxtehude chorales; oh, I didn't tell you about the kids. We have eleven of them now. Ann, Dot and I have one apiece, and Florence has eight. (But they're going to let me have quadruplets next week.) They let me take care of them pretty much for the first few weeks, while they're little, and they're *so* darling.

So mostly I spend my time taking care of the kids and working out tensor equations that Ski kindly gives me to do for him, and, I must confess it, feeling a little lonely. I *would* like to watch a TV quiz show over a cup of coffee with a friend! They let me do over the interior of our mobile home now and then. The other day I redid it in Pittsburgh suburban as a joke. Would you believe French windows in interstellar space? We never open them, of course, but they look real pretty with the chintz curtains and lace tiebacks. And we've added several new rooms for the children and their pets (Flo grew them the cutest little bunnies in the hydroponics plot).

Well, I've enjoyed this chance to gossip, so will sign off now. There is one thing I have to mention. The others have decided we don't want to get any more messages from you. They don't like the way you try to work on our subconsciouses and all (not that you succeed, of course, but you can see that it's still a little annoying), and so in future the dial will be set at six-six-oh, all right, but the switch will be in the "off" position. It wasn't my idea, but I was glad to go along. I *would* like some slightly less demanding company from time to time, although not, of course, yours.

Washington Five

Once upon a time the building that was now known as DoD Temp Restraining Quarters 7—you might as well call it with the right word, "jail," Knefhausen thought—had been a luxury hotel in the Hilton chain. The maximum security cells were in the underground levels, in what had been meeting rooms. There were no doors or windows to the outside. If you did get out of your own cell you had a flight of stairs to get up before you were at ground level, and then the guards to break through to get to the open. And then, even if there happened not to be an active siege going on at the moment, you took your chances with the roaming addicts and activists outside.

Knefhausen did not concern himself with these matters. He did not think of escape, or at least didn't after the first few panicky moments, when he realized he was under arrest. He stopped demanding to see the President after the first few days. There was no point in appealing to the White House for help when it was the White House that had put him here. He was still sure that if only he could talk to the President privately for a few moments he could clear everything up. But as a realist he had faced the fact that the President would never talk to him privately again.

So he counted his blessings.

First, it was comfortable here. The bed was good, the rooms were warm. The food still came from the banquet kitchens of the hotel, and it was remarkably good for jailhouse fare.

Second, the kids were still in space and still doing some things, great things, even if they did not report what. His vindication was still a prospect.

Third, the jailers let him have newspapers and writing materials, although they would not bring him his books or give him a television set.

He missed the books, but nothing else. He didn't need TV to tell him what was going on outside. He didn't even need the newspapers, ragged, thin and censored as they were. He could hear for himself. Every day there was the rattle of small-arms fire, mostly far-off and sporadic, but once or twice sustained and heavy and almost overhead, Brownings against AK-47s, it sounded like, and now and then the slap and smash of grenade launchers. Sometimes he heard sirens hooting through the streets, punctuated by clanging bells, and wondered that there was still a civilian fire department left to bother. (Or was it still civilian?) Sometimes he heard the grinding of heavy motors that had to be tanks. The newspapers did little to fill in the details, but Knefhausen was good at reading between the lines. The Administration was holed up somewhere—Key Biscayne or Camp David or Southern California, no one was saying where. The cities were all in red revolt. *Herr Omnes* had taken over.

For these disasters Knefhausen felt unjustly blamed. He composed endless letters to the President, pointing out that the serious troubles of the Administration had nothing to do with Alpha-Aleph; the cities had been in revolt for most of a generation, the dollar had become a laughingstock since the Indochinese wars. Some he destroyed, some he could get no one to take from him, a few he managed to dispatch—and got no answers.

Once or twice a week a man from the Justice Department came to ask him the same thousand pointless questions once again. They were trying to build up a dossier to prove it was all his fault, Knefhausen suspected. Well, let them. He would defend himself when the time came. Or history would defend him. The record was clear. With respect to moral issues, perhaps, not so clear, he conceded. No matter. One could not speak of moral questions in an area so vital to the search for knowledge as this. The dispatches from the *Constitution* had already produced so much!—although, admittedly, some of the most significant parts were hard to understand. The Gödel message had not been unscrambled, and the hints of its contents remained only hints.

Sometimes he dozed and dreamed of projecting himself to the *Constitution*. It had been a year since the last message. He tried to imagine what they had been doing. They would be well past the midpoint now, decelerating. The starbow would be broadening and diffusing every day. The circles of blackness before

and behind them would be shrinking. Soon they would
see Alpha Centauri as no man had ever seen it. To be
sure, they would then see that there was no planet called
Aleph circling the primary, but they had guessed that
somehow long since. Brave, wonderful kids! Even so
they had gone on. This foolishness with drugs and sex,
what of it? One opposed such goings-on in the common
run of humanity, but it had always been so that those
who excelled and stood out from the herd could make
their own rules. As a child he had learned that the
plump, proud air leader sniffed cocaine, that the great
warriors took their sexual pleasure sometimes with each
other. An intelligent man did not concern himself
with such questions, which was one more indication
that the man from the Justice Department, with his
constant hinting and prying into Knefhausen's own
background, was not really very intelligent.

The good thing about the man from the Justice Department was that one could sometimes deduce things
from his questions, and rarely—oh, very rarely—he
would sometimes answer a question himself. "Has there
been a message from the *Constitution?*" "No, of course
not, Dr. Knefhausen; now, tell me again, who suggested
this fraudulent scheme to you in the first place?"

Those were the highlights of his days, but mostly the
days just passed unmarked.

He did not even scratch them off on the wall of his
cell, like the prisoner in the Chateau d'If. It would
have been a pity to mar the hardwood paneling. Also,
he had other clocks and calendars. There was the tick-
ing of the arriving meals, the turning of the seasons as
the man from the Justice Department paid his visits.
Each of these was like a holiday—a holy day, not
joyous but solemn. First there would be a visit from
the captain of the guards, with two armed soldiers standing in the door. They would search his person and his

cell on the chance that he had been able to smuggle in
a—a what? A nuclear bomb, maybe. Or a pound of
pepper to throw in the Justice man's eyes. They would
find nothing, because there was nothing to find. And
then they would go away, and for a long time there
would be nothing. Not even a meal, even if a meal
time happened to be due. Nothing at all, until an hour
or three hours later the Justice man would come in
with his own guard at the door, equally vigilant inside
and out, and his engineer manning the tape recorders,
and his questions.

And then there was the day when the man from the
Justice Department came and he was not alone. With
him was the President's secretary, Murray Amos.

How treacherous is the human heart! When it has
given up hope, how little it takes to make it hope again!

"Murray!" cried Knefhausen, almost weeping, "it's
so good to see you again! The President, is he well?
What can I do for you? Have there been developments?"

Murray Amos paused in the doorway. He looked at
Dieter von Knefhausen and said bitterly, "Oh, yes,
there have been developments. Plenty of them. The
Fourth Armored has just changed sides, so we are
evacuating Washington. And the President wants you
out of here at once."

"No, no! I mean—oh, yes, it is good that the President is concerned about my welfare, although it is bad
about the Fourth Armored. But what I mean, Murray,
is this: Has there been a message from the *Constitution?*"

Amos and the Justice Department man looked at each
other. "Tell me, Dr. Knefhausen," said Amos silkily,
"how did you manage to find that out?"

"Find it out? How could I find it out? No, I only

asked because I hoped. There has been a message, yes? In spite of what they said? They have spoken again?"

"As a matter of fact, there has been," said Amos thoughtfully. The Justice Department man whispered piercingly in his ear, but Amos shook his head. "Don't worry, we'll be coming in a second. The convoy won't go without us. . . . Yes, Knefhausen, the message came through to Goldstone two hours ago. They have it at the decoding room now."

"Good, very good!" cried Knefhausen. "You will see, they will justify all. But what do they say? Have you good scientific men to interpret it? Can you understand the contents?"

"Not exactly," said Amos, "because there's one little problem the code room hadn't expected and wasn't prepared for. The message wasn't coded. It came in clear, but the language was Chinese."

Constitution Six

Ref.: CONSIX T51/11055/*7
CLASSIFIED MOST SECRET
Subject: Transmission from U. S. Starship *Constitution*.

The following message was received and processed by the decrypt section according to standing directives. Because of its special nature, an investigation was carried out to determine its provenance. Radio-direction data received from Farside Base indicate its origin along a line of sight consistent with the present predicted location of the *Constitution*. Strength of signal was high but within appropriate limits, and degradation of frequency separation was consistent with relativistic shifts and scattering due to impact with particle and gas clouds.

Although available data do not prove beyond doubt that this transmission originated with the starship, no contra-indications were found.

On examination, the text proved to be a phonetic transcription of what appears to be a dialect of Middle Kingdom Mandarin. Only a partial translation has been completed. (See note appended to text.) The translation presented unsuual difficulties for two reasons: One, the difficulty of finding a translator of sufficient skill who could be granted appropriate security status; two, because (conjecturally) the language used may not correspond exactly to any dialect but may be an artifact of the *Constitution's* personnel. (See PARA EIGHT, Lines 43-51 below, in this connection.)

This text is PROVISIONAL AND NOT AUTHEN-TICATED and is furnished only as a first attempt to translate the contents of the message into English. Efforts are being continued to translate the full message, and to produce a less corrupt text for the section herewith. Later versions and emendations will be forwarded when available.

TEXT FOLLOWS:

1 PARA ONE. The one who speaks for all [*Lt-Col*
2 *Sheffield H Jackman?*] rests. With righteous
3 action comes surcease from care. I [*identity*
4 *not certain, but probably Mrs Annette Marin*
5 *Becklund, less probably one of the other three*
6 *female personnel aboard, or one of their de-*
7 *scendants*] come in his place, moved by charity
8 and love.

9 PARA TWO. It is not enough to study or to do
10 deeds which make the people frown and bow
11 their heads. It is not enough to comprehend
12 the nature of the sky or the sea. Only through
13 the understanding of all can one approach wis-

14 dom, and only through wisdom can one act
15 rightly.
16 PARA THREE. These are the precepts as it is
17 given us to see them.
18 PARA FOUR. The one who imposes his will by
19 force lacks justice. Let him be thrust from a
20 cliff.
21 PARA FIVE. The one who causes another to
22 lust for a trifle of carved wood or a sweetmeat
23 lacks courtesy. Let him be restrained from the
24 carrying out of wrong practices.
25 PARA SIX. The one who ties a knot and says, "I
26 do not care who must untie it," lacks foresight.
27 Let him wash the ulcers of the poor and carry
28 nightsoil for all until he learns to see the day
29 to come as brother to the day that is.
30 PARA SEVEN. We who are in this here should
31 not impose our wills on you who are in that
32 here by force. Understanding comes late. We
33 regret the incident of next week, for it was
34 done in haste and in error. The one who
35 speaks for all acted without thinking. We who
36 are in this here were sorry for it afterward.
37 PARA EIGHT. You may wonder [*literally: ask
38 thoughtless questions of the hexagrams*] why
39 we are communicating in this language. The
40 reason is in part recreational, in part heuristic
41 [*literally: because on the staff hand one
42 becomes able to strike a blow more ably when
43 blows are struck repeatedly*], but the nature
44 of the process is such that you must go through
45 it before you can be told what it is. Our steps
46 have trodden this path. In order to reconstruct
47 the Chinese of the *I Ching* it was first neces-
48 sary to reconstruct the German of the trans-
49 lation from which the English was made. Error

50 lurks at every turn. [*Literally: false apparitions*
51 *shout at one each time the path winds*.] Many
52 flaws mark our carving. Observe it in silence
53 for hours and days until the flaws become part
54 of the work.
55 PARA NINE. It is said that you have eight days
56 before the heavier particles arrive. The dead
57 and broken will be few. It will be better if all
58 airborne nuclear reactors are grounded until
59 the incident is over.
60 PARA TEN. When you have completed rebuild-
61 ing send us a message, directed to the planet
62 Alpha-Aleph. Our home should be prepared
63 by then. We will send a ferry to help colonists
64 cross the stream when we are ready.

The above text comprises the first 852 groups of
the transmission. The remainder of the text, comprising
approximately 7500 groups, has not been satisfactorily
translated. In the opinion of a consultant from the
Oriental Languages Department at Johns Hopkins it
may be a poem.

/s/ Durward S RICHTER

Durward S RICHTER
Maj Gen USMC
Chief Cryptographer
Commanding

Distribution: X X X BY HAND ONLY

Washington Six

The President of the United States (Washington)
opened the storm window of his study and leaned out

60

to yell at his Chief Science Advisor. "Harry, get the lead out! We're waiting for you!"

Harry looked up and waved, then continued doggedly plowing through the dripping jungle that was the North Lawn. Between the overgrown weeds and the rain and the mud it was slow going, but the President had little sympathy. He slammed down the window and said, "Damn that man, he just goes out of his way to aggravate me. How long am I supposed to wait for him so I can decide if we're gonna have to move the capital or not?"

The Vice President looked up from her knitting. "Jimbo, honey, why do you fuss yourself like that? Why don't we just move and get it over with?"

"Well, it looks so lousy." He threw himself into a chair despondently. "I was really looking forward to the Tenth Anniversary parade," he complained. "Ten years, that's really worth bragging about! I don't want to hold it the hell out in the sticks, I want it right down Constitution Avenue, just like the old days, with the people cheering and the reporters and the cameras all over and everything. Then let that son of a bitch in Omaha say I'm not the real President."

His wife said placidly, "Don't fuss yourself about him, honey. You know what I've been thinking, though? The parade might look a little skimpy on Constitution Avenue anyway. It would be real nice on a kind of littler street."

"Oh, what do you know? Anyway, where would we go? If Washington's under water, what makes you think Bethesda would be any better?"

His Secretary of State put down his solitaire cards and looked interested. "Doesn't have to be Bethesda," he said. "I got some real nice land up near Dulles we could use. It's high there."

"Why, sure. Lots of nice land over to Virginia," the

Vice President confirmed. "Remember when we went out on that picnic after your Second Inaugural? That was at Fairfax Station. There was hills there all around. Just beautiful."

The President slammed his fist on the coffee table and yelled, "I'm not the President of Fairfax Station, I'm the President of the U. S. of A.! What's the capital of the U. S. of A.? Washington! My God, don't you see how those jokers in Houston and Omaha and Salt Lake and all would laugh if they heard I had to move out of my own capital?"

Be broke off, because his Chief Science Advisor was coming in the door, shaking himself, dripping mud as he got out of his oilskin slicker. "Well?" demanded the President. "What did they say?"

Harry sat down. "It's terrible out there. Anybody got a dry cigarette?"

The President threw him a pack. Harry dried his fingers on his shirt front before he drew one out. "Well," he said, "I went to every boat captain I could find. They all said the same. Ships they talked to, places they'd been. All the same. Tides rising all up and down the coast."

He looked around for a match. The President's wife handed him a gold cigarette lighter with the Great Seal of the United States on it, which, after some effort, he managed to ignite. "It don't look good, Jimmy. Right now it's low tide and that's all right, but it's coming in. And tomorrow it'll come in a little higher. And there's going to be storms, not just rain like this, I mean, but you got to figure on a tropical depression coming up from the Bahamas now and then."

"We're not in the tropics," said the Secretary of State suspiciously.

"It doesn't mean that," said the Science Advisor, who had once given the weather reports over the local

ABC television station, when there was such a thing as a television network. "It means storms. Hurricanes. But they're not the worst things; it's the tides. If the ice is melting then they're going to keep getting higher regardless."

The President drummed his fingers on the coffee table. Suddenly he shouted, "I don't *want* to move my capital!"

No one answered. His temper outbursts were famous. The Vice President became absorbed in her knitting, the Secretary of State picked up his cards and began to shuffle, the Science Advisor picked up his slicker and carefully hung it on the back of a door.

The President said, "You got to figure it this way. If we move out, then all those local yokels that claim to be the President of the United States are going to be just that much better off, and the eventual reunification of our country is going to be just that much more delayed." He moved his lips for a moment, then burst out, "I don't ask nothing for myself! I never have. I only want to play the part I have to play in what's good for all of us, and that means keeping up my position as the *real* President, according to the U. S. of A. Constitution as amended. And that means I got to stay right here in the real White House, no matter what."

His wife said hesitantly, "Honey, how about this? The other Presidents had like a Summer White House, and Camp David and like that. Nobody fussed about it. Why couldn't you do the same as they did? There's the nicest old farm house out near Fairfax Station that we could fix up to be real pretty."

The President looked at her with surprise. "Now, that's good thinking," he declared. "Only we can't move permanently, and we have to keep this place garrisoned so nobody else will take it away from us, and we have to come back here once in a while. How about that, Harry?"

His Science Advisor said thoughtfully, "We could rent some boats, I guess. Depends. I don't know how high the water might get."

"No 'guess'! No 'depends'! That's a national priority. We have to do it that way to keep that bastard in Omaha paying attention to the real President."

"Well, Jimbo, honey," said the Vice President after a moment, emboldened by his recent praise, "you have to admit they don't pay a lot of attention to us right now. When was the last time they paid their taxes?"

The President looked at her foxily over his glasses. "Talking about that," he said, "I might have a little surprise for them anyway. What you might call a secret weapon."

"I hope it does better than we did in the last war," said his wife, "because if you remember, when we started to put down the uprising in Frederick, Maryland, we got the pee kicked out of us."

The President stood up, indicating the Cabinet meeting was over.

"Never mind," he said sunnily. "You go on out again, Harry, and see if you can find any good maps in the Library of Congress where they got the fires put out. Find us a nice high place within, um, twenty miles if you can. Then we'll get the Army to condemn us a Summer White House like Mae says, and maybe I can sleep in a bed that isn't moldy for a change."

His wife looked worried, alerted by his tone. "What are you going to do, Jim?"

He chuckled. "I'm going to check out my secret weapon."

He shooed them out of his study and, when they were gone, went to the kitchen and got himself a bottle of Fresca from the six-pack in the open refrigerator. It was warm, of course. The Marine guard company was still trying to get the gas generator back in operation, but they were having little success. The President didn't mind. They were his personal Praetorians and, if they lacked a little as appliance repairmen, they had proved their worth when the chips were down. The President was always aware that during the Troubles he had been no more than any other Congressman—appointed to fill a vacancy, at that—and his rapid rise to Speaker of the House and Heir Apparent, finally to the Presidency itself, was due not only to his political skills and knowhow, but also to the fact that he was the only remotely legitimate heir to the Presidency who also happened to have a brother-in-law commanding the Marine garrison in Washington.

The President was, in fact, quite satisfied with the way the world was going. If he envied Presidents of the past (missiles, fleets of nuclear bombers, billions of dollars to play with), he certainly saw nothing, when he looked at the world around him, to compare with his own stature in the real world he lived in.

He finished the soda, opened his study door a crack and peered out. No one was nearby. He slipped out and down the back stairs. In what had once been the public parts of the White House you could see the extent of the damage more clearly. After the riots and the trashings and the burnings and coups, the will to repair and fix up had gradually dwindled away. The President didn't mind. He didn't even notice the charred walls and the fallen plaster. He was listening to the sound of a distant gasoline pump chugging away, and smiling to himself as he approached the underground level where his secret weapon was locked up.

The secret weapon, whose name was Dieter von Knefhausen, was trying to complete the total defense of every act of his life that he called his memoirs.

He was less satisfied with the world than the President. He could have wished for many changes. Better health, for one thing; he was well aware that his essential hypertension, his bronchitis, and his gout were fighting the last stages of a total war to see which would have the honor of destroying their mutual battleground, which was himself. He did not much mind his lack of freedom, but he did mind the senseless destruction of so many of his papers.

The original typescript of his autobiography was long lost, but he had wheedled the President—the pretender, that is, who called himself the President—into sending someone to find what could be found of them. A few tattered and incomplete carbon copies had turned up. He had restored some of the gaps as best his memory and available data permitted, telling again the story of how he had planned Project Alpha-Aleph and meticulously itemizing the details of how he had lied, forged and falsified to bring it about.

He was as honest as he could be. He spared himself nothing. He admitted his complicity in the "accidental" death of Ann Barstow's first husband in a car smash, thus leaving her free to marry the man he had chosen to go with the crew to Alpha Centauri. He had confessed he had known that the secret would not last out the duration of the trip, thus betraying the trust of the President who made it possible. He put it all in, all he could remember, and boasted of his success.

For it was clear to him that his success was already proved. What could be surer evidence of it than what had happened ten years ago? The "incident of next week" was as dramatic and complete as anyone could wish. If its details were still indecipherable, largely because of the demolition of the existing technology structure it had brought about, its main features were obvious. The shower of heavy particles—baryon? perhaps even quarks?—had drenched the Earth. The source had been traced to a point in the heavens identical with that plotted for the *Constitution*.

Also there were the messages received, and, take them together, there was no doubt that the astronauts had developed knowledge so far in advance of anything on Earth that, from two light-years out, they could impose their will on the human race. They had done it. In one downpour of particles, the entire military-industrial complex of the planet was put out of action.

How? How? Ah, thought Knefhausen, with envy and pride, that was the question. One could not know. All that was known was that every nuclear device—bomb, powerplant, hospital radiation source or stockpile—had simultaneously soaked up the stream of particles and at that moment ceased to exist as a source of nuclear energy. It was not rapid and catastrophic, like a bomb. It was slow and long-lasting. The uranium and the plutonium simply melted in the long, continuous reaction that was still bubbling away in the seething lava lakes where the silos had stood and the nuclear power plants had generated electricity. Little radiation was released, but a good deal of heat.

Knefhausen had long since stopped regretting what could not be helped, but wistfully he still wished he had the opportunity to measure the total heat flux properly. Not less than 10^{16} watt-years, he was sure, just to judge by the effects on the Earth's atmosphere, the storms, the gradual raising of temperature all over, above all by the rumors about the upward trend of sea level that bespoke the melting of the polar ice caps. There was no longer even a good weather net, but the fragmentary information he was able to piece together suggested a world increase of four, maybe as many as six or seven degrees Celsian already, and the reactions still seething away in Czechoslovakia, the Congo, Colorado, and a hundred lesser infernos.

Rumors about the sea level?

Not rumors, no, he corrected himself, lifting his head and staring at the snake of hard rubber hose that began under the duckboards at the far end of the room and ended outside the barred window, where the gasoline pump outside did its best to keep the water level inside his cell low enough to keep the water below the boards. Judging by the inflow, the grounds of the White House must be nearly awash.

The door opened. The President of the United States (Washington) walked in, patting the shoulder of the thin, scared, hungry-looking kid who was guarding the door.

"How's it going, Knefhausen?" the President began sunnily. "You ready to listen to a little reason yet?"

"I'll do whatever you say, Mr. President, but as I have told you there are certain limits. Also I am not a young man, and my health—"

"Screw your health and your limits," shouted the President. "Don't start up with me, Knefhausen!"

"I am sorry, Mr. President," whispered Knefhausen.

"Don't be sorry! What I got to judge by is results. You know what it takes to keep that pump going just so you won't drown? Gas is rationed, Knefhausen! Takes a high national priority to get it! I don't know how long I'm gonna be able to justify this continuous drain on our resources if you don't cooperate."

Sadly, but stubbornly, Knefhausen said: "As far as I am able, Mr. President, I cooperate."

"Yeah. Sure." But the President was in an unusually good mood today, Knefhausen observed with the prisoner's paranoid attention to detail, and in a moment he said: "Listen, let's not get uptight about this. I'm mak-

68

ing you an offer. Say the word and I'll fire that dumb son-of-a-bitch Harry Stokes and make you my Chief Science Advisor. How would that be? Right up at the top again. An apartment of your own. Electric lights! Servants—you can pick 'em out yourself, and there's some nice-looking little girls in the pool. The best food you ever dreamed of. A chance to perform a real service for the U. S. of A., helping to reunify this great country to become once again the great power it should and must be!"

"Mr. President," Knefhausen said, "naturally, I wish to help in any way I can. But we have been all over this before. I'll do anything you like, but I don't know how to make the bombs work again. You saw what happened, Mr. President. They're gone."

"I didn't say bombs, did I? Look, Kneffie, I'm a reasonable man. How about this. You promise to use your best scientific efforts *in any way you can.* You say you can't make bombs; all right. But there will be other things."

"What other things, Mr. President?"

"Don't push me, Knefhausen. Anything at all. Anything where you can perform a service for your country. You give me that promise and you're out of here today. Or would you rather I just turned off the pump?"

Knefhausen shook his head, not in negation but in despair. "You do not know what you are asking. What can a scientist do for you today? Ten years ago, yes. Even five years ago. We could have worked something out maybe; I could have done something. But now the preconditions do not exist. When all the nuclear plants went out— When the factories that depended on them ran out of power— When the fertilizer plants couldn't fix nitrogen and the insecticide plants couldn't deliver— When the people began to die of hunger and the pestilences started—"

"I know all that, Knefhausen. Yes or not?"

The scientist hesitated, looking thoughtfully at his adversary. A gleam of the old shrewdness appeared in his eyes.

"Mr. President," he said slowly. "You know something. Something has happened."

"Right," crowed the President. "You're smart. Now tell me, what is it I know?"

Knefhausen shook his head. After seven decades of vigorous life, and another decade of slowly dying, it was hard to hope again. This terrible little man, this upstart, this lump—he was not without a certain animal cunning, and he seemed very sure. "Please, Mr. President. Tell me."

The President put a finger to his lips, and then an ear to the door. When he was convinced no one could be listening, he came closer to Knefhausen and said softly:

"You know that I have trade representatives all over, Knefhausen. Some in Houston, some in Salt Lake, some even in Montreal. They are not always there just for trade. Sometimes they find things out, and tell me. Would you like to know what my man in Anaheim has just told me?"

Knefhausen did not answer, but his watery old eyes were imploring.

"A message," whispered the President.

"From the *Constitution?*" cried Knefhausen. "But, no, it is not possible! Farside is gone, Goldstone is destroyed, the orbiting satellites are running down—"

"It wasn't a radio message," said the President. "It came from Mount Palomar. Not the big telescope, because that got ripped off too, but what they call a Schmidt. Whatever that is. It still works. And they still have some old fogies who look through it now and then, for old times' sake. And they got a message, in laser light. Plain Morse code. From what they said was Alpha Centauri. From your little friends, Knefhausen."

He took a sheaf of paper from his pocket and held it up.

Knefhausen was racked by a fit of coughing, but he managed to croak: "Give it to me!"

The President held it away. "A deal, Knefhausen?"

"Yes, yes! Anything you say, but give me the message!"

"Why, certainly," smiled the President, and passed over the much-creased sheet of paper. It said:

PLEASE BE ADVISED. WE HAVE CREATED THE PLANET ALPHA-ALEPH. IT IS BEAUTIFUL AND GRAND. WE WILL SEND OUR FERRIES TO BRING SUITABLE PERSONS AND OTHERS TO STOCK IT AND TO COMPLETE CERTAIN OTHER BUSINESS. OUR SPECIAL REGARDS TO DR. DIETER VON KNEFHAUSEN, WHOM WE WANT TO TALK TO VERY MUCH. EXPECT US WITHIN THREE WEEKS OF THIS MESSAGE.

Knefhausen read it over twice, stared at the President and read it again. "I—I am very glad," he said inadequately.

The President snatched it back, folded it and put it in his pocket, as though the message itself was the key to power. "So you see," he said, "it's simple. You help me, I help you."

"Yes. Yes, of course," said Knefhausen, staring past him.

"They're your friends. They'll do what you say. All those things you told me that they can do—"

"Yes, the particles, the ability to reproduce, the ability, God save us, to build a planet—" Knefhausen might have gone on cataloguing the skills of the spacemen indefinitely, but the President was impatient:

"So it's only a matter of days now, and they'll be here. You can imagine what they'll have! Guns, tools, everything—and all you have to do is get them to join me in restoring the United States of America to its proper place. I'll make it worth their while, Knefhausen! And yours, too. They—"

The President stopped, observing the scientist carefully. Then he cried "Knefhausen!" and leaped forward to catch him.

He was too late. The scientist had fallen limply to the duckboards. The guard, when ordered, ran for the White House doctor, who limped as rapidly to the scene as his bad legs and brain soaked with beer would let him, but he was too late too. Everything was too late for Knefhausen, whose old heart had failed him . . . as it proved a few days later (when the great golden ships from Alpha-Aleph landed and disgorged their bright, terrible crewmen to clean up the Earth), just in time.

Sad Solarian Screenwriter Sam

In a personal sense it may seem unfortunate that the entire population of the planet Earth was sentenced to death. One had, after all, a certain sense of justice. One looks for a quality that could be called mercy. One thinks that there is really some hope that soon or late the present itchy, brawling species would be replaced by something nobler and more kind, and it seems a pity to foreclose that chance. And above all one demurs at the principle of the champion. Is it right that tigers and tortoises, too, should die because of the sins of the human beast to which they are only vaguely related? Is it even right that three-plus billions of humans should be put away on the basis of a close study of only one individual? Not fair, one thinks. But as one of the greatest of the Great Ones caused to be encoded, it isn't a fair space-time continuum, and in the long run one must face the fact that, fair or not, mankind has had it. The total destruction of all has been ordered and is on its way.

Nevertheless, it is of some historical interest to preserve a record of the process by which the human race was condemned.

At that era, which was in the 8×10^{23} time unit after the Monobloc, certain subsidiary intelligences had been assigned as proctors to the planets of a GO star, with particular attention to the planet locally called

Earth. It was not a very nice planet, but it had picked up the trick of photosynthesis and oxygen was infiltrating its atmosphere and it needed study.

The duty of these intelligences was dull, but they were dull, too. They didn't notice that it was dull. They watched the courses of their nine orbiting planets for a while, spoke among themselves, drowsed, estivated in standby mode, and woke to watch again. If anything, they rather liked it. They had hardship privileges, so that when they were in active mode they could inhale delightful intoxicating gases and eat various delicacies, including, as population allowed, each other. Mostly they estivated in their clay packs, for many sequences of 10^{19} units, while on their planets the usual events occurred. Mountains rose. Seas dried. Great beasts trumpeted through steamy swamps.

Ultimately the event for which they were programmed to watch occurred. In one such sequence the process called "technology" began to appear on one of their planets, and when next one of the intelligences roused itself to scan solar space, it detected an artifact in orbit.

At once all were awakened and set about their specialized tasks.

In mere 10^7s of time units they had completed a synoptic study along the lines laid down by Those Who had appointed them to this work. This caused them some terror. The records indicated that there had been a good many artifacts in orbit in recent 10^9s, but they had failed to observe them because of their estivation and a deorbited positron in one of the automatic warning devices. It was some comfort to them that nearly all of the artifacts had been cislunar to Earth, and none had been transsolar, which would have really pulled the cork on everything. But it became evident that approximate intelligence had developed on three, possibly four, of the bodies in their solar system, and so it was with gnawing apprehension that they prepared to shift from observing to action modes.

When the action leader had completed his decision-making process, he assumed command status and emanated, "Individual report."

This was known to be the procedure They had ordered, and so all accepted it. The subordinate whose duty it was to carry out such commands transponded a query: "Which individual?"

This required additional decision-making, so all waited while the leader analyzed the indications. To do so properly, it found it necessary to examine into many 10^5s of factors, including geographic dispersal, hereditary characteristics, and state of awareness of the artifact now approaching Earth. The criteria They had programmed were simple sampling techniques in the main, so that the leader did not need to call on specialized help. It isolated three choices, all of which were optimal. One was a Party apparatnik in a suburb of Bucharest. One was a sweeper in Benares. The third was a motion-picture scenarist in Southern California. Following Their procedures for tie-breaking, the leader gamed an arbitrary choice and extruded a filament of indications: "That one."

"That one" was five feet three inches tall and twenty-seven years old. He was wholly unaware that he had been chosen to stand for all life on Earth, or even that he was being watched. He was driving his Capri from his agent's home on Gower to The World's Biggest Drugstore, practicing racing starts at the lights and listening to the disk jockies on the car radio, when he achieved the state of awareness that made him eligible to represent humanity. He didn't know that that had happened. He only knew that he had heard something crazy in a news break. The crazy thing was that the Algonquin Nine spacecraft was on its way back from Mars, and it was bringing three real live Martians with it.

Sam Harcourt, as he was called, immediately fell into a study. Martians. He knew all about Martians, although to be sure he hadn't thought much about them since the age of thirteen. But he remembered all those marvelous old stories, and it came to him as the light turned green and the driver of the semi-trailer behind him began to blow his horn, that that knowledge had a cash value to him right then. He scooted across the intersection as the light changed again, pulled over into a No Parking zone, set the handbreak, and phoned his agent. "Jesus R. Christ, Oleg," he shouted when the phone was answered, "have I got an idea. *Barsoom*."

His agent's voice was thinly patient. "I wish you wouldn't keep calling me up, Sam. You're supposed to be seeing Chavez."

"I've got plenty of time to see Chavez, and anyway this is probably too big for him. His art-nudies are all out the window now. Don't you know? Don't you ever turn on your radio, watch TV, open the door and listen to what people are talking about? It's Martians. They found live Martians, and they're bringing them back!"

The agent said, "Yes, I did hear something." Cautiously: "What about it?"

"I want to do a film about Barsoom, Oleg. That's the native name for Mars. Do you see the potential? I thought at first of one of the majors, but they're too slow, they'd miss the exploitation. It has to be now. A gorgeous red-skinned Martian princess. A big aerial fight, like the Battle of Britain, only with swords. Comedy. Sex! Oleg," cried Sam into his car phone, watching the police car that was moving slowly toward him along the Strip, "I have to hang up in a minute, but you haven't heard the best part. This isn't a Sam Harcourt original. It's a classic that every boy has read, and the beauty is, it's maybe in the public domain, because somebody didn't renew the copyrights."

"Maybe, Sam?"

"Well," said Sam, "I remember something about it. It was some time ago, but your legal department could check it out."

"My legal department," said the agent, "gets a hundred and a half every time I ask him a question and I have better questions to ask him than did somebody forget to renew a copyright. Anyway, you forgot something, too. Please let me remind you. Daniel Chavez made a special trip in from the Valley to hear what you're going to write for him and, Sam, please, Chavez is eight thousand dollars cash, a guaranteed sale once it gets past the front office. Come out of the clouds, Sam, with your twenty million dollars' worth of public domain. If it's public domain what have you got to sell anyway?"

"That's what I have an agent for," said Sam. "Call you back." And he hung up, released the brake and was in motion, nodding pleasantly to the driver of the black-and-white before it reached him.

The subordinate proctor meditated for a few 10s of units in some concern. It was bred to be both conscientious and obedient, and it had never before encountered a situation in which its conscience conflicted with its obedience. In a sense peculiar to its species, it disliked Sam Harcourt very much.

It reached a decision and withdrew rapidly to report. "Preference for selecting an alternative specimen for evaluation?" it wheedled.

The leader was outraged. "Negative," it rapped.

Although the subordinate was far too well programmed to quarrel with a decision, something inside it stuck at the prospect of condemning one hundred billion vertebrates and tens of trillions of lesser breeds, down to the blue-green algae, on the basis of an evaluation of Sam Harcourt. "Personal discomfort," it complained, and offered, "Recommendation for alternative proctor?"

The leader assumed command mode.

"Return for continuation *or* prospect of disciplinary action," it stated disjunctively, and with what passed in its species for a sigh the subordinate proctor rejoined Sam.

To art films Daniel Chavez was what Mack Sennett had been to comedy. He was fast and cheap.

He had not always specialized in art films. His first big b.o. success, *Monster of the Maelstrom,* had been a sci-fic shocker shot principally in his backyard swimming pool, which had a center-draining plug. Counting his profits, he saw that this was a magic money machine and looked for fuel to keep it running. It happened that his next-door neighbor was a collie breeder. One morning, listening to the yelps from the next yard and remembering some unused special-effects footage that was already paid for, Daniel Chavez came up with his next triumph, *Laddie Meets the Maelstrom Monster.* He then sensed that sci-fic had had its day and moved on. He successively rode the crest of the surfer wave, flew with the drug scene, bared all in the nudies and arrived, home free, in the art film, a most congenial environment since hand-held cameras, finance-wise, were a lot more attractive than even rented studio space. One of his principles was low overhead. He saw no reason to maintain an office while there were booths in cafeterias and soda fountains.

As Sam Harcourt came into The World's Biggest Drug Store, Chavez was casting his next picture. "You'll do, my dear," he said, patting the ass of a young girl in hip-huggers as she rose from the seat beside him. "Don't forget, I'll pick you up so we can go over your characterization. Around nine-thirty," he explained, "because I have a business dinner date." She peered impassively at Harcourt through two feet of frizzy hair and slouched away.

Harcourt took her seat and said for openers, "Chavez, *cinema verité* is dead."

"Funny you should say that," said Chavez. "I agree with you. I'm putting that kid in my next picture: *Up Against the Wall, Cardinal McIntyre!* I think it has the potential of a modern *The Devils*."

"How would she look in brick-red body makeup, Chavez?"

"No, no. She's playing a young nun who wants to be relevant."

"No, good," said Harcourt. "Relevant flicks are out. I'm talking about Martians."

"Oh, my God," said Chavez, looking at him with loathing, "I told Oleg I didn't want any more crap from you. I didn't even want to talk to you, but he said you had a fresh approach."

"That was then. I did. You would have loved it. But now I've got something better."

Chavez sighed. "Hold it while I get something to drink. You want a vanilla malted?" He half rose, looking for the waitress.

"Chocolate. I guess you didn't hear, so I have to tell you. It was on the radio. The astronauts checked in. They're coming back from Mars, and they've got real live Martians with them. And what I have to offer you today is a story about Martians that, with any luck at all, you can have in release before they're out of quarantine."

Chavez sat down again. He stroked his sideburns, looking at Sam, who rushed on:

"Real Martians, Chavez! Authentic. Timely. I'm not talking about crappy monster stuff, I'm talking about the big one you've been getting ready for all your life."

Chavez had begun to shake his head. "You know what that process stuff costs?" But he was listening.

"Who said process? Now it can be real Martians. Everybody's talking about it. I'm actually astonished you haven't heard."

Chavez meditated for a moment, rousing himself as the waitress came by. "Two malteds, honey, one black, one white. Sam, I like it a little bit."

"Not just a little bit. You like it a lot."

"I like it well enough to ask you how you're going to get them signed up. Do they speak English, do you know?"

"We can dub it. Listen, let me tell you the story. The man is a war hero. He's trapped in a cave with Indians—no, wait a minute, with Viet Cong soldiers waiting outside. They kill him. He goes outside, and —we'll call him John Carter—and Carter stares up at the stars, and he sees this one big star, Mars. He stretches out his arms to it. Do you see any big cost so far?"

"I don't even see any story so far, Sam. Why do you want to call him 'John Carter'? I'd like a better name— Rick Carstairs?"

Elated, Harcourt cried: "That's great. So Carstairs stretches out his arms and somehow, mysteriously, he's drawn to Mars. Right out of his body. Right into space, *pssssschwt*, zooming past the stars, and all of a sudden we cut to him falling to the ground on Mars, and this great big ugly Martian is poking him with a sword. So

Cart—so Carstairs jumps up, and he jumps right over the big boy. This is kind of a tricky technical point to grasp, but on Mars he can jump like crazy because—"

"Sam," chided Chavez, "don't you remember I produced *Worlds at War?* You don't have to explain that sort of thing to me. They're on a planet beyond the pull of gravity, so go on."

"Right, Chavez! So they have this terrible sword fight, and Carstairs is winning, and along comes another Martian, green this time, with four arms—no," he said hastily as Chavez began to scowl, "it could be only two arms in a regular Martian suit, if you don't want too much special effects, and Carstairs licks them all, and rescues their girl prisoner. She's beautiful, Chavez! Red. Maybe that kid could play her. Her name is Dejah, wait a minute, Dejah Thoris. She says, 'Ikky-pikky Hoo-hah Barsoom?' Carstairs says, 'I don't understand your words, madam, but in tribute to your loveliness I cast my sword at your feet.' And he does. Well, she blushes. He doesn't know why, but—what's the matter?"

"I don't get something there. You said she was red-skinned, right? How can you tell she's blushing?"

Sam hesitated. The waitress brought their malteds, and he unzipped his straws from their wrapper and took a long sip before he answered. "A good point," he said. "I think I can handle it, but let's pass it for now. Anyway, she picks up his sword and hands it to him, and then she acts like she's waiting for something, but he doesn't know what. Some other Martians come at them, and he picks her up and jumps the hell away with her over the roof of the breeding shed—I didn't tell you that part. They're near a breeding shed where these green Martians lay their eggs. That's only a detail, but there's good values in it. Comedy. Maybe there's this one Martian that's a sort of a butterfingers, and he drops this egg, and it's his own little boy—"

Chavez finished his malted, wiped his lips and said courteously, "Let's pass that part about the eggs for now, too, although I ought to say I think it stinks."

"Well, anyway. So then Carter and the girl get away and there's a hell of a big aerial battle—what is it?"

Chavez waggled a finger. "Carter, Sam?"

"Yeah, Carstairs. But then is the big part. An aerial battle in the thin air of dying Mars! This is the only place where you'll need a lot of process stuff, but it's going to be worth it. And, listen, I have an idea that could help out with the money part. How'd you like to get the whole shooting script for nothing? I mean, not a nickel, Chavez, except maybe a few grand to cover expenses—maybe not even that," he said hastily, watching Chavez's face. "Let's say even no cash at all, just a cut of the producer's net."

Chavez's lips were compressed now, the fingertips of his joined hands pressed against them in thought. He parted the fingers far enough to ask, "How big a cut, Sam?"

"We'll work it out. Hell. Even fifteen percent. I don't care, as long as it makes a good picture—twelve and a half, maybe," he amended. "I'd frankly prefer not to discuss money with you. Oleg doesn't like his clients doing that."

"Yeah. I know what Oleg doesn't like." Chavez stroked his left sideburn very hard for a moment. Then he pulled back his coat sleeve to examine the Accutron on his hairy wrist and said, "I'll be open with you, Sam, and tell you that with costs the way they are now, that kind of deal could put me right through the wringer. Still, maybe we can work something out. Not on those lines, exactly."

Sam protested, "I was only trying to help with front

money. Anyway, they win the battle and take the girl back to her father, he's a local king, and then Carstairs sees there's something wrong. The girl's gone all sort of mad and crying, and her father's scowling and fingering his ray-gun. What'd he do? The father says, 'Huppeta-huppeta cranberries!' and it looks like there's going to be another fight but then the girl, he's taught her a little English by now, she says, 'Rick, I can't figure you out' and he says, 'Why, what's the matter?' and then it comes out. That business where he threw the sword in front of her? On Mars, that's like a proposal of marriage, and when he didn't follow through that's like treating her like a tramp. So anyway they clear that up and—and that's all. Clinch. Music up and out. Final bit of comedy with this pet mind-reading kind of dog she's got. Chavez," he said earnestly, "I can see every frame of this film. I only hope I've been able to make you see it too."

Chavez meditatively sipped the last of his ice water. He said, "Sam. I like it."

"A little bit, Chavez?"

"More than a little bit, Sam. I got to think. Also I've got to dig a little more about these Martians. But—"

He shrugged winningly, smiled and beckoned the waitress. He offered her his American Express card to cover the two malteds, the two earlier iced teas, and the cheese Danish he'd split with the girl. "Let me sleep on it," he said. "I'll call Oleg in the morning. I mean that, Sam. Don't go telling him to call me up the minute you get out of here. It's possible there's something there so don't crap it up." And they parted, each, in his way, well pleased.

It was not within the competence of a subordinate proctor to make decisions. Once, their race, too, had been under the scrutiny of Those Who ordered the

Galaxy, and although they had passed and been allowed to continue, subject, of course, to certain modifications and improvements, ancestral fear remained. The proctor which returned from its tasks of monitoring Sam felt some empathy and concern. Its projections pointed clearly toward an inevitable conclusion. It would not make the decision, but it had a pretty clear notion of what the decision would be.

Sentients like Sam were rare in the Galaxy, because They did not care to tolerate weeds in Their garden.

On hearing the report, the leader activated its decision-making systems and came to a conclusion, which it stated in the form of an imperative: "Verify by means of making a prediction and observing its occurrence," it instructed them, in the manner of what even humans knew as "the scientific method."

"Description of prediction?" interrogated the subordinates.

"Prediction based on observation and analysis: Specimen will exhibit no manifestations of creativity, compassion,   ,   or   within the next 10^7 time units." (The three omitted terms do not have equivalents in human languages.)

"Recommendation if verified?"

The leader hesitated slightly. "Randomization of all organic matter of this system," it proposed.

This conclusion was not lightly reached. It was not that the proctors gave, as they would have said, a quark's emission for the human race, or even for the Martians which were even at that moment landing at Kennedy Spaceport. It was not even that they felt sympathy for a race condemned to die. Their concern was more personal. The task of randomizing all organic matter in even this trivial solar system, thus destroying all its life and giving it a fresh start, would be most arduous and time-consuming. Their opportunities for estivation would be very slim while it was going on.

Moreover, there was a certain apprehension. It was known that Those Who mandated them rather enjoyed cuddly pets. It had seemed that there was some hope of discovering some new creatures of that sort for Them in this system, for at the time of the last inspection the highest primate on Earth had been Oreopithecus, a creature which was hairy, tree-living, four-footed and, in a sense which Those Who had put them there appreciated, rather cute. It was disappointing that Oreopithecus had developed into Sam. The projections of the proctors included some probability of displeasure on Their part over the negligence that had let that evolution take place.

Nevertheless their duty was clear, and each of the subordinate decision-makers, reviewing the evidence, concurred: "Agreed."

The necessity of the leader's decision was clearly in accord with Their directions. Therefore the subordinate proctors lined up before the leader, extended the spurs on each of their twenty-four feet, and kicked it to death, as was their right. When they had finished eating, a new leader assumed the responsibility of implementing their decision.

Sam's mind was glowing with thoughts of screen credits and residuals as he drove out of the parking lot and around the corner. He ducked into a Phillips 66 filling station, waved away the pump attendant as he parked, and picked up the phone.

"Now what, for the Christ sake?" asked the agent irritably when Sam had identified himself. "Don't tell me. Chavez laughed in your face and you want me to find you another live one, right?"

Sam chortled, "You couldn't be wronger, he's

hooked. H. O. O, ooked, hooked. He practically promised fifteen percent of the net, in fact. I count on you to firm up the details."

There was silence on the phone, except for the raspberry noise of static from someone somewhere racing his car engine. Sam grinned. "You having a heart attack, Oleg? Surprised I pulled off a deal you couldn't make in a million years?"

Cautiously, "I have to admit," the agent said, "that I didn't really anticipate this outcome, exactly. When you say 'practically guaranteed,' Sam, exactly how practically?"

"Come on, Oleg. The details are your problem, right? That's what you always tell me: 'Let me put on the screws, dummy.' But he didn't say no."

"Yeah, bullshit, boy." But the agent's tone was reluctantly admiring.

"You'll call him?"

The agent rallied his skepticism, which had always served him well "Maybe I'll call him. I already called some people. You've got a little problem you don't know about. That 'Barsoom' stuff? I talked to a fellow that knows, and they straightened out that copyright matter."

"Christ, Oleg," howled Sam, "if you blew this deal—"

"What blew? It's all on the record, no problem. I'm just telling you that it isn't public domain, like you thought."

"All right," cried Sam, refusing to come down. "What can it cost? Offer them fifty th— Offer them twenty-five percent of my take. Five hundred dollars for an option. They'll go for it. If you're the contracts man you tell me you are, they will. Anyway," he said, picking up speed, "this is only for openers. What do we need Chavez for? If Chavez'll go for it, maybe Paramount will go. Cosby. Kubrick. With the values this thing has

got, capitalizing on a hundred million dollars' worth
of free publicity—"

"Yeah, yeah!" Oleg interrupted. "Look at him! One
'maybe' from a Daniel Chavez and he's telling me the
agency business." But his tone was not hostile. In
fact, it was definitely ingratiating. "All right, Sam. We're
in this together and I'll roll the dice with you. And
listen, I've got something that can help out. You know
Dorfman, the naturalist? Best seal man in the country.
Used to train for Marineland of the Pacific. Well, I
happen to have the representation for him."

"Hold it there a minute," said Sam. An unreasoning
panic began to seep into his veins. "Oleg, why are you
telling me about this crappy animal act?"

"I mean, for your Martians."

"I don't get what you're talking about."

'Well, Sam. Maybe you can't get the real ones, right?
But I see an angle. I was just looking at the pictures
on TV. Take away those fnnny little arms and the
teeth, and what have you got? A regular seal. Now,
if there's anybody who can dress up a seal to look like
a Martian I assure you, Sam, this Dorfman is—"

"Oleg!" screamed Sam.

There was a pause. "Oh," said the agent. "You
mean you didn't see what they look like yet?" Another
pause. Then, with the normal irritation back in his
voice, the agent said, "Sam, look, I got a meeting.
Tell you what you do. Go home and turn on a TV
set and look at your Martians, then call me back.
If you've got anything to call me about.

The new leader of the team of proctors dabbled fret-
fully with the mud of its estivation hutch, considering
certain disagreeable aspects of its own future. When the
subordinate returned, the leader received its report
on the behavior of the subject human in silence.

The other proctors waited for its response. They did not wait patiently, since they had never been impatient. They simply waited.

At length the leader announced its findings: "Prediction confirmed. Model verified. Subject race does not conform to minimum requirements."

The subordinate proctors murmured among themselves.

The leader assumed command mode: "Instructions: Preparation of synoptic report. Recommendation to randomize. Transmission of data and recommendation to—" He did not complete the sentence, only raised several of his eyes to look upward.

The subordinate proctors proceeded at once to their various duties. Those charged with such matters prepared holographic representations of Sam Harcourt and of a number of humans associated with him, including the sweeper in Benares and the Rumanian party functionary; of assorted Terrestrial artifacts which they thought They would find interesting, including the *Queen Elizabeth II,* an Atlas Five booster rocket, and a transistor radio; of the Martians which were now staring sluggishly, with cowlike eyes, at the TV cameras in the briefing room of Patrick A.F.B., just south of Kennedy Spaceport. They included many subsidiary bits of evidence, such as a demographic map of Mars, showing the primitive villages the voyagers had left, as well as a number of Martian artifacts. Their basic list completed, they paused to consider what else might be of value. It was a question of some importance. Assuming Those Who appointed them followed the recommendation, and it was unthinkable They would not, this omnium-gatherum would stand through all eternity as the only surviving record of the then-vanished creatures of the solar system of Earth. At length they choose to reproduce some drawings of jockstraps and Bikini briefs from a Sears-Roebuck catalogue and the entire contents of Leningrad's Hermitage museum, and considered their work done.

At that point those charged with encoding information into packets of binary bits did so, and those charged with transmission began to reorient their vessel, as it swung in its long orbit between Mercury and Saturn, and prepared to send.

And so a pulsed series of message-bearing particles leaped into space, traveling at the speed of light toward the place where Those Who directed them had Their locus of existence.

The message stated, fully and fairly—to the extent that those concepts had meaning in the minds of Those Who guided the Galaxy or Their servants—all that was needful to be said about mankind.

From then on, the process would be automatic and inevitable. The recommendation to destroy all life in the solar system would be passed on by higher-order intelligences to the Highest of all, and except for the unlikely event of Their deciding to reverse the recommendations of Their subordinates, the command to proceed would be returned at once.

Life would be destroyed. Earth, Mars, South Polar Venus and Ganymede, the four sites now known to possess authochthonous intelligent life of some degree, would be the first to be randomized, but all the rest would follow, down to the least formaldehyde radical in the farthest solar gas cloud. The planets of the sun would wheel along, bare and ready for a fresh start. Bombay and Beverly Hills would be one with Nineveh and Tyre.

The bean the sampling machine had popped out for testing sat in front of his 27-inch TV screen, staring with rage and loathing at what he saw. A forgotten glass of soda water had gone warm and flat in his hand.

Seals? The Martians were not even seals. He glared at them in full living color, the picture as sharp as eighteen hundred dollars and a community antenna could make it, and hated them. With everything the network technicians could do going for them, on the screen of the best television set in Brentwood Heights, they looked like big, charcoal-gray slugs.

"Dejah Thoris," sobbed Sam. "The *bastards.*"

If only they had just been ugly— If only they had just been strange— What they were was nasty, disgusting and dull.

Sam Harcourt set down the glass of soda, snapped the remote button and let the picture fade away. With it went all his dreams of red-skinned beauties and battles in the Barsoomian skies. After a long time, he complained to the blank screen: "Why couldn't you at least look like *something?*"

But they couldn't. The Martians had evolved to fit an environment orders of magnitude harsher than our own. They were slow, dull and hideous not because they wanted to be, but because they could not be anything but what their environment made them. Any more than could Sam Harcourt.

And while he sat there, the message carrying Earth's death sentence sped out across the plane of the ecliptic, toward a point in the constellation of Sagittarius, where an intertwined looping of stars in a fanciful arrangement lay half across the Galaxy from Earth.

While Sam was phoning his agent from the Phillips 66 gas station, the message was already crossing the orbit of Mars. Before he reached home it leaped the asteroid belt and the orbit of Jupiter. It passed Saturn while his television set was warming up, approached

Uranus as he sat staring at his fate, launching itself toward the orbits of Neptune and Pluto, and beyond.

The proctors, murmuring among themselves, returned to estivation, getting ready for the demands that would be made on them when the reply to their message was received and the hard work of ending life on all the sun's planets would begin. They would be grateful then for all the rest they could store up, although in truth there was plenty of time to rest.

The abode of Those Who ruled them, on and around the planets that floated among their various stars, was thirty-one thousand light years away, by Earthly measurements. Thirty-one thousand years it would take for the message to get there, thirty-one thousand years more for the response to come back. The sentence was passed. The date for the execution was set. In the year 64,000 A.D., give or take a century or two, humanity's day would be done.

Call Me Million

To look at Charley DiSalle, who is I, you would think him not much. For instance, the you who was BeauLee Cartworth thought he was a snoring drunk. The you who were Mr. and Mrs. Ripton R. Gilvey saw him vomiting and wheezing over the wall around Hyde Park. "He's an American," said the male of you charitably. The female said, "He's the kind of American we left Titusville to avoid. Let's go." But you didn't go far, did you? Not that you were so very much yourselves, Mr. and Mrs. G. You were a snack to be consumed and forgotten, Diet-Rite people, not much nourishment in you.

But Charley DiSalle is not unfair, and he admits he wasn't much to look at, even then. Now he's worse. He's fat and fifty. The backs of his hands are covered with little brown blots. His face looks as though he'd just waked up. He would dress nicely if he could, but he forgets.

You can't reasonably blame him for any of this, because he can't help growing old, and he has a lot on his mind. As you should know, of course, all of you.

When Charley DiSalle was slim and twenty, sideburns down to his earlobes and duck-ass hair, they drafted him. Shaved the back of his neck. Gave him a gun. Charley was not in any way hip or wild, and he

97

certainly could not be described as political. When they sent him to Nam the thing that made him hate it was wholly this: He did not want his own only self to get killed.

He must admit now, looking back thirty years at the little scared kid jumping rustily out of the Globemaster into the heat of Tan Son Nhut, that he could have handled it in a different way. He could have got himself a break. He was just too dumb, young and innocent to think of feeling a master sergeant up or getting caught with grass or anything like that. Smarter and older, he could have got himself into Public Information or some headquarters job. He wasn't that smart. What he decided to do was desert. On his first forward search-and-destroy mission he lagged back, threw away his weapon and ducked off the trail. He remembers how scared and detached it felt while he was sitting there, waiting for the V.C. to come out and collect his surrender.

The time passed and passed. He heard what he thought were snakes and felt what he knew were bugs. Charley wet his pants that night, especially when shooting started a few hundred yards away.

But he stayed there. And stayed. And just before dawn he blinked, and opened his eyes, and there was the little brown man standing there with a knife in his hand. But it wasn't Charley's surrender he wanted. It was his life.

Scared? You know Charley was scared. The V.C. touched him with one hand while he drew back the knife in his other, and that was the first that Charley ate.

Now, a thousand or ten thousand tasty tidbits later, he can still remember the sharp, glad, sweaty taste of that one. The empty V.C. straightened up and walked stumbling away, with what mattered of him left behind in Charley DiSalle. Charley can't tell you exactly what it was like. He thinks it must be, in a way, something like being pregnant, holding encompassed inside you that other life that is not your life. Or he thinks it could be something like writing a play. You know? With all the Romeos and Juliets and Mercutios roaming loose around the inside of your mind, not existing at all except through you? But what it was mostly like was swallowing a great big jolt of something mellow and fine.

Do you, any of you, get to share that feeling when it happens with someone new? Charley can't tell. He can't feel what you feel. He reaches inside to touch you now and then, and finds some of you stolid and stunned, some wailing, some what-the-hell. But what you think or feel beyond that he cannot say.

So he decided maybe after all he wouldn't have to desert, went thoughtfully back to the rendezvous, and they let him out of the Army a few months later. Tried to hang a drug rap on him, finally busted him out on a Section 8. It was a great trouble for them to figure that one out. All Charley's enemies died. They went staggering away after he ate them (which, of course, no one knew he had done or could have believed), and what was left of them seldom lived an hour. It was very bad for unit morale. But how could they stop him? And where in the regulations does it say you shouldn't do what Charley did? Nowhere. They gave up and threw him out.

There were good years then. Money? Charley had all the money he wanted out of the pockets and purses of those he ate. Women? It was the easiest thing in the world to get women. He just asked. Sometimes they said no to what he asked for, but one way or another he always got something he wanted. Friends? Well, no, that was not so good. He had no friends. There was no way for Charley to have friends, considering how much he had to move around. But he wasn't precisely lonely, as one might define what it is to be lonely, in the sense that he lacked on-going companionship with a peer group. Dears, he always had you.

And you, and you, and you. One at a time, five at a time, sometimes more. On a Union Pacific sleeper he ate a whole car, and jumped off in the morning while the porter lunged and stumbled blankly down the aisle. He nibbled a whole class out of a black nursery school near Nashville, four-year-olds and fives. They were bland and sweet and not frightened. On the car ferry from Zadar across the Adriatic he lured a plump Jug blonde to his stateroom, had her and then had her again in a way that astonished her; then, one by one, he ate the dozen or so Italian youths who were showing off their muscles by the ship's pool; the girls who had been pretending not to see them; the purser who sold him the stateroom, and half the crew. The ship came charging full speed into Ancona with its whistle blasting in terror and Charley had to jump over the side and swim ashore, so great was the alarm; whereafter he tried to be more discreet. Those years! Those endless treats! Hollywood hippies and Roman whores and a taxi driver in a fog in Berkeley Square. High over the planalto he ate a Varig purser, sweet and slow, staring out the window all the time while the crimson rivers below turned ochre, then mauve, and joined the blue of the lakes. A floor waiter in Venice, Italy, a beachful of kids in Venice, California. An Intourist girl in Leningrad and a cable-car man on Powell Street. He loved you all dearly, each of you and all of you; but there was always such a fuss. So much noise and panic. Such headlines in the papers, such cries on the TV.

Interpol chased him and the Security Council debated

him, but he was too incredible to be in much danger from the pursuit of rational men. No one could understand what was going on. Least of all, Charley DiSalle.

But he tried; give him credit for that, he tried.

He tried to find out what he was and whether he was unique. Before he ate the red-haired librarian at the Bibliotheque Nationale, he queried her for hours. He inquired of a monk at the Vatican museum. He spent a week with a mescal-eater in Yucatan. None of them could tell him anything that it was of any use to know. He ate them all.

Money kept silting up in his pockets, and he found a use for it other than buying plane tickets and paying hotel bills. He banked some, built up an identity, wrote letters. A magazine editor gave him the name of a psychologist in Honolulu, and Charley retained him for consultation, a thousand dollars on the line and two hundred dollars a day, the price high because his letters were so queer. They arranged to meet in the lobby of a hotel on Waikiki, because Charley was wary of receptionists who remembered faces. Charley can see him now as he approached, his eyes closed, his head resting against an ironwood carving, an ambiguously dressed American professional wearing a jacket from Rome, a shirt from London, and socks that didn't match. He looked asleep, but Charley saw that his fingers were tapping, tapping. "Don't be nervous," said Charley, and the man opened his eyes and said, "I'm the one who says things like that. Sit."

Now, what Charley did was put the whole thing to him as a hypothetical question. Probably the psychologist recognized that old gambit right away. Of course he did. He sat there watching Charley's temples pulse, and he smiled to himself. But it must have been a problem to him, and perhaps he came to believe it was no gambit after all, since Charley's situation had to sound so very hypothetical. Or did he believe that it was all true? In any case he was hired and he earned his pay. He listened without arguing all the way through, and then he said, "No, sir. What you describe is not recorded in the literature. There is no case of anyone who lives by absorbing other people's personalities. Or souls, if you prefer. Like a vampire, you mean? No. On the other hand, do you mean the existence of multiple personalities in one mind? Yes, speaking loosely, in lay terms, such things do exist. They do not come about by the transfer of personality from one person to another, but I can tell you about them if that is what you want to know." Charley listened patiently to all the man had to say, but it turned out that it wasn't what he wanted to know at all. The psychologist had never heard of anything like that; went back and searched the literature, for an additional fee, and still had never heard of it. It was disheartening, and when Charley ate him at last he did not enjoy it much.

Poor Charley, poorest Charley, he was so alone, and he hated it so. Or so he thought at the time. But how much more he hated it when, a little later on, he found out he was not, after all, entirely unique.

Well, Charley cannot ask *you* to feel sorry for him about that. As a mater of fact, not even I can feel really sorry for him, although I am he. For all that was ten years gone or more, and now as he roams the dwindling world he feels those others somewhere around. In Denver a waitress in a coffee shop stumbled out from behind her counter and died; she had been eaten, but not by Charley. Those stories in the paper about Nairobi and the reports from Red China— Charley had never been in Africa, never been in China; those terrors were not him. And then when the stories stopped, because newspapers stopped, the victims began to appear first here, then there, then more and more: Charley thinks he saw one like himself, in the Greyhound station in Boston, and he is sure that he has been seen.

All these years they've been avoiding each other, all the children that grew to be Charleys. But how many there must now be. There is only the one measure of it, and that is how few there are left to eat. It cannot be long now, that time when all you edibles are gone and the Charleys turn to each other. What an hour that will be, when Charley meets another like himself, and the casual snack turns out to be a devourer too; and when he dies he'll scream, I think, with all your million throats.

Shaffery Among the Immortals

Jeremy Shaffery had a mind a little bit like Einstein's, although maybe not in the ways that mattered most. When Einstein first realized that light carried mass he sat down to write a friend about it and described the thought as "amusing and infectious." Shaffery would have thought that, too, although of course he would not likely have seen the implications of the Maxwell equations in the first place.

Shaffery looked a little bit like Einstein. He encouraged the resemblance, especially in the hair, until his hair began to run out. Since Einstein loved sailing, he kept a sixteen-foot trimaran tied up at the Observatory Dock. Seasickness kept him from using it much. Among the things he envied Einstein for was the mirror-smooth Swiss lakes, so much nicer than the lower Caribbean in that respect. But after a day of poring over pairs of star photographs with a blink comparator or trying to discover previously unknown chemical compounds in interstellar space in a radio trace, he sometimes floated around the cove in his little yellow rubber raft. It was relaxing, and his wife never followed him there. To Shaffery that was important. She was a difficult woman, chronically p.o.'d because his career was so persistently pointed in the wrong direction. If she had ever been a proper helpmeet, she wasn't anymore. Shaffery doubted she ever had, remembering that it was her unpleasant comments that had caused him to give up that other hallmark of the master, the violin.

At the stage in Shaffery's career at which he had become Director of the Carmine J. Nuccio Observatory in the Lesser Antilles he had begun to look less like Einstein and more like Edgar Kennedy. Nights when the seeing was good he remorselessly scanned the heavens through the 22-inch reflector, hoping against hope for glory. Days when he was not sleeping he wandered through the dome like a ghost, running his finger over desks for dust, filching preserved mushrooms from Mr. Nuccio's home-canned hoard, trying to persuade his two local assistants to remember to close the dome slit when it rained. They paid little attention. They knew where the muscle was, and that it wasn't with Shaffery. He had few friends. Most of the white residents couldn't stand his wife; some of them couldn't stand Shaffery very well, either. There was a nice old lady drunk out from England in a tidy white house down the beach, a sort of hippie commune on the far side of the island, and a New York television talk-show operator who just flew down for weekends. When they were respectively sober, unstoned and present, Shaffery sometimes talked to them. That wasn't often. The only one he really wanted to see much was the tv man, but there were obstacles. The big obstacle was that the tv man spent most of his waking time skin-diving. The other obstacle was that Shaffery had discovered the tv man occasionally laid Mrs. Shaffery; it wasn't the morality of the thing that bothered him, it was the feeling of doubt it raised in Shaffery's mind about the other's sanity. He never spoke to the tv man about it, partly because he wasn't sure what to say and partly because the man had halfway promised to have Shaffery on his show. Sometime or other.

One must be fair to Shaffery and say that he wasn't a bad man. Like Frank Morgan, his problem was that he wasn't a good wizard. The big score always evaded him.

The Einstein method, which he had studied assiduously over many years, was to make a pretty theory and then see if, by any chance, observations of events in the real world seemed to confirm it. Shaffery greatly approved of that method. It just didn't seem to work out for him. At the Triple A-S meeting in Dallas he read an hour-long paper on his new principle of Relevance Theory. That was a typical Einstein idea, he flattered himself. He had even worked out simple explanations for the lay public, like Einstein with his sitting on a hot stove or holding hands with a pretty girl. "Relevance Theory," he practiced smiling to the little wavelets of the cove, "only means that observations that don't *relate* to anything don't *exist*. I'll spare you the mathematics because"—self-deprecatory laugh here— "I can't even fill out my income tax without making a mistake." Well, he had worked out the mathematics, inventing signs and operators of his own, just like Einstein. But he seemed to have made a mistake. Before the AAAS audience, fidgeting and whispering to each other behind their hands, he staked his scientific reputation on the prediction that the spectrum of Mars at its next opposition would show a slight but detectable displacement of some 150 Angstroms toward the violet. The son of a bitch didn't do anything of the kind. One of the audience was a graduate student at Princeton, hard up for a doctoral thesis subject, and he took a chance on Shaffery and made the observations, and with angry satisfaction sent him the proof that Mars had remained obstinately red.

The next year the International Astrophysical Union's referees, after some discussion, finally allowed him twenty minutes for a Brief Introduction into the General Consideration of Certain Electromagnetic Anomalies. He offered thirty-one pages of calculations leading to the prediction that the next lunar eclipse would be forty-two seconds late. It wasn't. It was right on time. At the meeting of the World Space Science Symposium they told him with great regret that overcommitments of space and time had made it impossible for them to schedule his no doubt valuable contribution, and by the time of the next round of conferences they weren't even sending him invitations any more.

Meanwhile all those other fellows were doing great. Shaffery followed the careers of his contemporaries with rue. There was Hoyle, still making a good thing out of the Steady State Hypothesis, and Gamow's name, still reverenced for the Big Bang, and new people like Dyson and Ehricke and Enzmann coming along with all sorts of ideas that, if you looked at them objectively, weren't any cleverer than his, Shaffery thought, except for the detail that somehow or other they seemed lucky enough to find supporting evidence from time to time. It did not strike him as fair. Was he not a Mensa member? Was he not as well educated as the successful ones, as honored with degrees, as photogenic in the newsmagazines and as colorfully entertaining on the talk shows? (Assuming Larry Nesbit ever gave him the chance on his show.) Why did they make out and he fall flat? His wife's theory he considered and rejected. "Your trouble, Jeremy," she would say to him, "is you're a horse's ass." But he knew that wasn't it. Who was to say Isaac Newton wasn't a horse's ass, too, if you looked closely enough at his freaky theology and his nervous breakdowns? And look where he got.

So Shaffery kept looking for the thing that would make him great. He looked all over. Sometimes he checked Kepler's analysis of the orbit of Mars with an adding machine, looking for mistakes in arithmetic. (He found half a dozen, but the damn things all canceled each other out, which proves how hard it is to go wrong when your luck is in.) Sometimes he offered five-dollar prizes to the local kids for finding new stars that might turn out to be Shaffery's Nova, or anyway Shaffery's Comet. No luck. An ambitious scheme to describe stellar ballistics in terms of analogy with free-radical activity in the enzyme molecules fell apart when none of the biochemists he wrote to even answered his letters.

The file of failures grew. One whole drawer of a cabinet was filled with reappraisals of the great exploded theories of the past—*A New Look at Phlogiston*, incomplete because there didn't seem really to be anything to look at when you came down to it; a manuscript called *The Flat Earth Reexamined*, which no one would publish; three hundred sheets of drawings of increasingly tinier and increasingly quirkier circles to see if the Copernican epicycles could not somehow account for what the planet Mercury did that Einstein had considered a proof of relativity. From time to time he was drawn again to attempting to find a scientific basis for astrology and chiromancy, or predicting the paths of charged particles in a cloud chamber by means of yarrow stalks. It all came to nothing. When he was really despairing he sometimes considered making his mark in industry rather than pure science, wherefore the sheaf of sketches for a nuclear-fueled car, the experiments on smellovision that had permanently destroyed the nerves of his left nostril, the attempt to preserve some of Mr. Nuccio's mushrooms by irradiation in his local dentist's X-ray room. He knew that that sort of thing was not really worthy of a man with all those graduate degrees, but in any event he did no better there than anywhere else. Sometimes he dreamed of what it would be like to run Mount Palomar or Jodrell Bank, with fifty trained assistants to nail down his inspirations with evidence. He was not that fortunate. He had only Cyril and James.

It was not all bad, however, because he didn't have much interference to worry about. The observatory where he was employed, last and least of the string of eleven that had given him a position since his final doctoral degree, didn't seem to mind what he did, as long as he did it without bothering them. On the other hand, they didn't give him much support, either.

Probably they just didn't know how. The observatory was owned by something called the Lesser Antilles Vending Machine Entertainment Co., Ltd., and, so Shaffery had been told by the one old classmate who still kept up a sort of friendship with him, was actually some sort of tax-evasion scheme maintained by a Las Vegas gambling syndicate. Shaffery didn't mind this, particularly, although from time to time he got tired of being told that the only two astronomers who mattered were Giovanni Schiaparelli and Galileo Galilei. That was only a minor annoyance. The big cancerous agony was that every year he got a year older and fame would not come.

At his periodic low spots of despondency (he had even tried linking them with the oppositions of Jupiter, meteor showers, and his wife's periods, but those didn't come to anything either) he toyed with the notion of dropping it all and going into some easier profession. Banking. Business Law. "President Shaffery" had the right kind of sound, if he entered politics. But then he would drag his raft to the water, prop two six-packs of Danish beer on his abdomen and float away, and by the end of the first pack his courage would come flowing back, and on the second he would be well into a scheme for detecting gravity waves by statistical

analysis of 40,000 acute gout sufferers, telephoning the
state of their twinges into a central computer facility.

On such a night he carried his little rubber raft
to the shore of the cove, slipped off his sandals, rolled
up his bellbottoms and launched himself. It was the
beginning of the year, as close to winter as it ever
got on the island, which meant mostly that the dark
came earlier. It was a bad time of the year for him,
because it was the night before the annual Board
Meeting. The first year or two he had looked forward to
the meetings as opportunities. He was no longer so
hopeful. His objective for the present meeting was only
to survive it, and there was some question of a nephew
by marriage, an astronomy major at *U.C.L.A.*, to
darken even that hope.

Shaffery's vessel wasn't really a proper raft, only the
sort of kid's toy that drowns a dozen or so nine-year-
olds at the world's bathing beaches every year. It
was less than five feet long. When he got himself
twisted and wriggled into it, his back against the
ribbed bottom, his head pillowed against one inflated
end and his feet dangling into the water at the other, it
was quite like floating in a still sea without the annoyance of getting wet. He opened the first beer and
began to relax. The little waves rocked and turned him;
the faint breeze competed with the tiny island tide, and
the two of them combined to take him erratically away
from the beach at the rate of maybe ten feet a minute.
It didn't matter. He was still inside the cove, with
islandlets, or low sandbanks, beaded across the mouth of
it. If by any sudden meteorological miracle a storm
should spring from that bright-lamped sky, the wind
could take him nowhere but back to shore or near an
island. And of course there would be no storm. He
could paddle back whenever he chose, and as easily as

he could push his soap dish around his bathtub, as he routinely did while bathing—which in turn he did at least once a day, and when his wife was particularly difficult, as often as six times. The bathroom was his other refuge. His wife never followed him there, being too well brought up to run the chance of inadvertently seeing him doing something filthy.

Up on the low hills he could see the corroded copper dome of the observatory. A crescent of light showed that his assistant had opened the dome, but the light showed that he was not using it for any astronomical purpose. That was easy to unriddle. Cyril had turned the lights on so that the cleaning woman could get the place spotless for the Board Meeting, and had opened the dome because that proved the telescope was being used. Shaffery bent the empty beer can into a V, tucked it neatly beside him in the raft, and opened another. He was not yet tranquil, but he was not actively hurting anywhere. At least Cyril would not be using the telescope to study the windows of the Bon Repos Hotel across the cove, since the last time he'd done it he had jammed the elevating gears and it could no longer traverse anywhere near the horizon. Shaffery put aside an unwanted, fugitive vision of Idris, the senior and smartest cleaning lady, polishing the telescope mirror with Bon Ami, sipped his beer, thought nostalgically of Relevance Theory and how close he had come with the epicycles, and freed his mind for constructive thought.

The sun was wholly gone, except for a faint luminous purpling of the sky in the general direction of Venezuela. Almost directly overhead hung the three bright stars of Orion's Belt, slowly turning like the traffic signals on a railroad line, with Sirius and Procyon orbiting headlight bright around them. As his eyes dark-adapted he could make out the stars in Orion's sword, even the faint patch of light that was the great gas cloud. He was far enough from the shore so that sound could not carry, and he softly called out the great four-pointed pattern of first magnitude stars that surrounded the constellation: "Hey there, Betelguese. Hi, Bellatrix. What's new, Rigel? Nice to see you again, Saiph." He glanced past red Aldebaran to the close-knit stars of the Pleiades, returned to Orion and, showing off now, called off the stars of the Belt: "Hey Alnitak! Yo, Alnilam! How goes it, Mintaka?"

The problem with drinking beer in the rubber raft was that your head was bent down toward your chest and it was difficult to burp, but Shaffery arched his body up a little, getting some water in in the process but not caring, got rid of the burp, opened another beer, and gazed complacently at Orion. It was a satisfying constellation. It was satisfying that he knew so much about it. He thought briefly of the fact that the Arabs had called the Belt Stars by the name Jauzah, meaning the Golden Nuts; that the Chinese thought they looked like a weighing beam; and that Greenlanders called them Siktut, The Seal-Hunters Lost at Sea. As he was going on to remember what the Australian aborigines had thought of them (they thought they resembled three young men dancing a corroboree), his mind flickered back to the lost seal-hunters. Um, he thought. He raised his head and looked toward the shore.

It was now more than a hundred yards away. That was farther than he really wanted to be, and so he kicked the raft around, oriented himself by the stars and began to paddle back. It was easy and pleasant to do. He used a sort of splashy upside-down breast stroke of the old-fashioned angel's wing kind, but as all his weight was supported by the raft he moved quickly across the water. He was rather enjoying the exercise, toes and fingers moving comfortably in the tepid sea, little ghosts of luminescence glowing where he splashed, until quite without warning the fingertips of one hand struck sharply and definitely against something that was resistently massive and solid where there should have been only water, something that moved stubbornly, something that rasped them like a file. Oh, my God, thought Shaffery. What a lousy thing to happen. They so seldom came in this close to shore. He didn't even think about them. What a shame for a man who might have been Einstein to wind up, incomplete and unfulfilled, as shark shit.

He really was not a bad man, and it was the loss to science that was first on his mind, only a little later what it must feel like to be chopped and gulped.

Shaffery pulled his hands in and folded them on his chest, crossed his feet at the ankles and rested them on the end of the boat, knees spread on the sides. There was now nothing trailing in the water that might strike a shark as bait. There was, on the other hand, no good way for him to get back to shore. He could yell, but the wind was the wrong way. He could wait till he drifted near one of the islets. But if he missed them he would be out in the deep ocean before he knew it.

Shaffery was almost sure that sharks seldom attacked a boat, even a rubber one. Of course, he went on analytically, the available evidence didn't signify. They could flip a raft like this over easily enough. If this particular shark ate him off this particular half-shell there would be no one to report it.

Still, there were some encouraging considerations. Say it was a shark. Say it was capable of tipping the boat or eating him boat and all. They were dull-witted creatures, and what was to keep one hanging around in the absence of blood, splashing, noise, trailing objects, or any of the other things sharks were known to take an interest in? It might be a quarter mile away already. But it wasn't, because at that moment he heard the splash of some large object breaking the surface a foot from his head.

Shaffery could have turned to look, but he didn't; he remained quite motionless, listening to the gentle water noises, until they were punctuated by a sort of sucking sound and then a voice. A human voice. It said, "Scared the piss out of you, didn't I? What do you say, Shaffery? Want a tow back to shore?"

It was not the first time Shaffery had encountered Larry Nesbit diving in the cove, it was only the first time it had happened at night. Shaffery twisted about in the raft had gazed at Nesbit's grinning face and its frame of wet strands of nape-length hair. It took a little time to make the transition in his mind from eighteen-foot shark to five-foot-eight TV star. "Come on," Nesbit went on, "what do you say? Tell you what. I'll tow you in, and you give me some of old Nuccio's Scotch, and I'll listen to how you're going to invent anti-gravity while we get pissed."

That Nesbit, he had a way with him. The upshot of it all was that Shaffery had a terrible hangover the next day; not the headache but the whole works, with trotting to the toilet and being able to tolerate only small sips of ginger ale and wishing, or almost wishing, he was dead. (Not, to be sure, before he did the one immortalizing thing. Whatever it was going to be.)

It was not altogether a disaster, the hangover. The next morning was very busy, and it was just as well that he was out of the way. When the Board of Directors convened to discuss the astronomical events of the year, or whatever it is they did discuss in the afternoon session to which Shaffery was definitely not invited, it was always a busy time. They arrived separately, each director with his pair of associates. One after another,

40-foot cabin cruisers with fishing tops came up to the landing and gave up cargoes of plump little men wearing crew cuts and aloha shirts. The observatory car, not ever used by any of the observatory personnel, was polished, fueled and used for round trips from the landing strip at Jubila, across the island, to Coomray Hill and the observatory. Shaffery laid low in his private retreat. He had never told his wife that he was not allowed in the observatory for the Board Meetings, so she didn't look for him. He spent the morning in the tarpaper shack where photographic material had once been kept, until he discovered that the damp peeled the emulsion away from the backing. Now it was his home away from home. He had fitted it with a desk, chair, icebox, coffepot and bed.

Shaffery paid no attention to the activity outside, not even when the Directors' assistants, methodically searching the bushes and banana groves all around the observatory, came to his shack, opened the door without knocking and peered in at him. They knew him from previous meetings, but they studied him silently for a moment before the two in the doorway nodded to each other and left him again. They were not well mannered men, Shaffery thought, but no doubt they were good at their jobs, whatever those jobs were. He resolutely did not think about the Board Meeting, or about the frightening, calumnious things Larry Nesbit had said to him the night before, drinking the Board Chairman's Scotch and eating his food, in that half-jocular, shafting, probing way he had. Shaffery thought a little bit about the queasy state of his lower abdomen, because he couldn't help it, but what he mostly thought about was Fermat's Last Theorem.

A sort of picayune, derivative immortality was waiting there for someone. Not much, but Shaffery was getting desperate. It was one of those famous mathematical problems that grad students played at for a month or two, and amateurs assaulted in vain all their lives. It looked easy enough to deal with. It started with so elementary a proposition that every high-school boy mastered it about the time he learned to masturbate successfully. If you squared the sides of a right triangle, the sum of the squares of the two sides was equal to the square of the hypotenuse.

Well, that was all very well, and it was so easy to understand that it had been used to construct right angles by surveyors for centuries. A triangle whose sides were, say, 3 feet and 4 feet, and whose hypotenuse was 5 feet, had to make a right angle, because $3^2 + 4^2 = 5^2$, and it always had, since the time of Pythagoras, five hundred years B.C. $a^2 + b^2 = c^2$. The hitch was, if the exponent was anything but 2, you could never make the equation come out using whole numbers, $a^3 + b^3$ never equaled c^3, and $a^{27} + b^{27}$ did not add up to any c^{27}, no matter what numbers you used for a, b and c. Everybody knew that this was so. Nobody had ever proved that it *had* to be so, by mathematical proofs, except that Fermat had left a cryptic little note, found among his papers after his death, claiming that he had found a "truly wonderful" proof, only there wasn't enough room in the margin of the book he was writing on to put it all down.

Shaffery was no mathematician. But that morning, waking up to the revolution in his stomach and the thunder in his head, he had seen that that was actually a strength. One, all the mathematicians of three or four centuries had broken their heads against the problem, so obviously, it couldn't be solved by any known mathematics anyway. Two, Einstein was weak in mathematics too, and had disdained to warry about it, preferring to invent his own.

So he spent the morning, between hurried gallops

across the parking lot to the staff toilet, filling paper with mathematical signs and operators of his own invention. It did not seem to be working out, to be sure. For a while he thought of an alternative scheme, to wit, inventing a "truly wonderful" solution of his own and claiming he couldn't find room to write it down in the margin of, say, the latest issue of *Mathematical Abstracts;* but residual sanity persuaded him that perhaps no one would ever find it, if it was found it might well be laughed off, and anyway that was purely posthumous celebrity and he wanted to taste it while he was alive. So he broke for lunch, came back feeling dizzy and ill and worried about the meeting that was going on, and decided to take a nap before resuming his labors.

When Cyril came looking for him to tell him the Directors desired his presence, it was dark, and Shaffery felt like hell.

Coomray Hill was no taller than a small office building, but it got the mirror away from most of the sea-level dampness. The observatory sat on top of the hill like a mound of pistachio ice cream, hemispheric green copper roof and circular walls of green-painted plaster. Inside, the pedestal of the telescope took up the center of the floor. The instrument itself was traversed as low as it would go any more, clearing enough space for the Directors and their gear. They were all there, looking at him with silent distaste as he came in.

The inner sphere of the dome was painted (by Cyril's talented half-sister) with a large map of Mars, showing Schiaparelli's famous canals in resolute detail; a view of the Bay of Naples from the Vomero, with Vesuvius gently steaming in the background; and an illuminated drawing of the constellation Scorpius, which happened to be the sign of the constellation under which the Chairman of the Board had been born. A row of card-tables had been lined up and covered with a green cloth. There were six places set, each with ashtray, note pad, three sharpened pencils, ice, glass, and bottle of John Begg. Another row of tables against the wall held the antipasto, replenished by Cyril after the depredations of the night before, but now seriously depleted by the people for whom it was intended. Six cigars were going and a couple of others were smoldering in the trays. Shaffery tried not to breathe. Even with the door open and the observing aperture in the dome wide, the inside air was faintly blue. At one time Shaffery had mentioned diffidently what the deposit of cigar smoke did to the polished surface of the 22-inch mirror. That was at his first annual meeting. The Chairman hadn't said a word, just stared at him. Then he nodded to his right-hand man, a Mr. DiFirenzo, who had taken a packet of Kleenex out of his pocket and tossed it to Shaffery. "So wipe the goddam thing off," he had said. "Then you could dump these ashtrays for us, okay?"

Shaffery did his best to smile at his Directors. Behind him he was conscious of the presence of their assistants, who were patrolling the outside of the observatory in loose elliptical orbits, perigeeing at the screen door to peer inside. They had studied Shaffery carefully as he came across the crunching shell of the parking lot, and under their scrutiny he had decided against detouring by way of the staff toilet, which he now regretted.

"Okay, Shaffery," said Mr. DiFirenzo, after glancing at the Chairman of the Board. "Now we come to you."

Shaffery clasped his hands behind him in his Einstein pose and said brightly, "Well, it has been a particularly productive year for the Observatory. No doubt you've seen my reports on the Leonid meteorite count and—"

"Right," said Mr. DiFirenzo, "but what we been talking about here is the space shots. Mr. Nuccio has expressed his views that this is a kind of strategic location, like how they shoot the rockets from Cape Kennedy. They have to go right over us, and we want a piece of that."

Shaffery shifted his weight uneasily. "I discussed that in my report last year—"

"No, Shaffery. This year, Shaffery. Why can't we get some of that federal money, like for tracking, for instance?"

"But the position hasn't changed, Mr. DiFirenzo. We don't have the equipment, and besides NASA has its own—"

"No good, Shaffery. You know how much you got out of us for equipment last year? I got the figures right here. And now you tell us you don't have what we need to make a couple bucks?"

"Well, Mr. DiFirenzo, you see, the equipment we have is for purely scientific purposes. For this sort of work you need quite different instruments, and actually—"

"I don't want to hear." DiFirenzo glanced at the Chairman, and then went on. "Next thing, what about that comet you said you were going to discover?"

Shaffery smiled forgivingly. "Really, I can't be held accountable for that. I didn't actually say we'd *find* one. I merely said that the continuing *search* for comets was part of our basic *program*. Of course, I've done my very best to—"

"Not good enough, Shaffery. Besides, your boy here told Mr. Nuccio that if you did find a comet you wouldn't name it the Mr. Carmine J. Nuccio comet like Mr. Nuccio wanted."

Shaffery was going all hollow inside, but he said bravely: "It's not wholly up to me, is it? There's an astronomical convention that it is the discoverer's name that goes on—"

"We don't like that convention, Shaffery. Three, now we come to some really bad things, that I'm sorry to hear you've got yourself into, Shaffery. We hear you been talking over the private affairs of this institution and Mr. Nuccio with that dick-head Nesbit. Shut, Shaffery," the man said warningly as Shaffery started to open his mouth. "We know all about it. This Nesbit is getting himself into big trouble. He has said some very racist things about Mr. Nuccio on that sideshow of his on the TV, which is going to cost him quite a bundle when Mr. Nuccio's lawyers get through with him. That is very bad, Shaffery, and also, four, there is this thing."

He lifted up what had seemed like a crumpled napkin in front of his place. It turned out that it was covering what looked like a large transistor radio.

Shaffery identified it after a moment's thought; he had seen it before, in Larry Nesbit's possession. "It's a tape recorder," he said.

"Right on, Shaffery. Now the question is, who put it in here? I don't mean just left it here like you could leave your rubbers or something, Shaffery. I mean left it here with one of those trick switches so it was going when a couple of our associates checked the place out and found it under the table."

Shaffery swallowed very hard, but even so his voice sounded unfamiliar to him when he was able to speak. "I—I *assure* you, Mr. DiFirenzo! I had nothing to do with it."

"No, Shaffery, I know you didn't, because you are not that smart. Mr. Nuccio was quite upset about this illegal bugging, and he has already made some phone calls and talked to some people and we have a pretty good idea of who put it there, and he isn't going to have what he thinks he's going to have to play on his TV show. So here it is, Shaffery. Mr. Nuccio doesn't find your work satisfactory here, and he is letting you go. We got somebody else coming down to take over. We'd appreciate it if you could be out by tomorrow."

There are situations in which there is not much scope for dignity. A man in his middle fifties who has just lost the worst job he ever had has few opportunities for making the sort of terminal remark that one would like to furnish one's biographers.

Shaffery discovered that he was worse off than that; he was frankly sick. The turmoil in his belly grew. The little saliva pumps under his tongue were flooding his mouth faster than he could swallow, and he knew that if he didn't get back to the staff toilet very quickly he would have another embarrassment to add to what was already an overwhelming load. He turned and walked away. Then marched. Then ran. When he had emptied himself of everything in belly, bladder and gut, he sat on the edge of the toilet seat and thought of the things he could have said: "Look, Nuccio, you don't know anything about science." "Nuccio, Schiaparelli was all wrong about the canals on Mars." It was too late to say them. It was too late to ask the question that his wife would be sure to ask, about severance pay, pension, all the things that he had been putting off getting in writing. ("Don't worry about that stuff, Shaffery, Mr. Nuccio always takes care of his friends but he don't like to be aggravated.") He tried to make a plan for his future, and failed. He tried even to make a plan for his present. Surely he should at least call Larry Nesbit, to demand, to complain and to warn ("Hist! The tape recorder has been discovered! All is lost! Flee!"), but he could not trust himself so far from the toilet. Not at that exact moment. And a moment later it was too late. Half an hour later, when one of the orbiting guards snapped the little lock and peered inside, the man who might have been Einstein was lying on the floor with his trousers around his knees, undignified, uncaring, and dead.

Ah, Shaffery! How disappointed he would have been in his *Times* obit, two paragraphs buried under the overhang of a pop singer's final notice. But afterward. . . .

The first victim was Larry Nesbit, airsick in his Learjet all the way back to New York, overcome during the taping of his TV show and dying the next day. The next victims were the Board of Directors, every man. They started home, by plane and boat. Some of them made it, but all of them died: en route or in Las Vegas, Detroit, Chicago, Los Angeles, New York, and Long Branch, New Jersey. Some of the "assistants" died and some were spared. (Briefly.) The reason was not a mystery for very long. The source of the new plague was tracked down quickly enough to Mr. Nuccio's antipasto, and particularly to the preserved mushrooms that Shaffery had borrowed for his experiment.

The botulinus toxin was long recognized as the most deadly poison known to man. The mutated version that Shaffery and his dentist's X-rays had brought into being was not much more deadly, but it had another quality that was new and different. Old, established botulinus clostridium is an organism with a feeble hold on life; expose it to light and air, and it dies. B. shafferia was more sturdy. It grew where it was. In anything. In Mr. Nuccio's antipasto, in a salad in a restaurant kitchen, in Mom's apple pie on a windowsill to cool, in the human digestive tract. There were nine deaths in the first five days, and then for a moment no more. The epidemiologists would not have bothered their heads about so short a casualty list if it had not been for the identities of some of the victims. But the bacteria were multipling. The stain of vomit under the boardwalk at Long Branch dried; the bacteria turned into spores and were blown on the wind until they struck something damp and fertile. Whereupon they grew. The soiled Kleenex thrown from a Cadillac Fleetwood on the road leading from O'Hare to Evanston, the sneeze between flights at Miami, expectorations in a dozen places—all added to the score. From the urine and feces of the afflicted men, from their sweat, even from their bed linen and discarded clothing, enspored bacteria leaped into the air and were inhaled, eaten, drunk, absorbed into cuts, in every way ingested into the waiting bodies of hundreds, then thousands, ultimately countless millions of human beings.

By the second week Detroit and Los Angeles were declared disaster areas. By the fourth the plague had struck every city in America, and had leaped the oceans. If it had any merciful quality at all, it was that it was quick: an upset stomach, a sweat, a few pangs and then death. None were immune. Few survived. Out of a hundred, three might outlive the disease. But then famine, riot, and lesser ills took their toll; and of the billions who lived on the Earth when Shaffery exposed his antipasto in the dentist's office, all but a few tens of millions died in the outbreak that the world will never forget of the disease called Shaffery's Syndrome.

The Merchants of Venus

I

My name, Audee Walthers. My job, airbody driver. My home, on Venus, in a Heechee hut most of the time; wherever I happen to be when I feel sleepy otherwise.

Until I was twenty-five I lived on Earth, in Amarillo Central mostly. My father, a Deputy Governor of Texas. He died when I was still in college, but he left me enough dependency benefits to finish school, get a master's in business administration, and pass the journeyman examination for clerk-typist. So I was set up for life.

But, after I tried it for a few years, I discovered I didn't like the life I was set up for. Not so much for the conventional reasons; I don't mind smog suits, can get along with neighbors even when there are 800 of them to the square mile, tolerate noise, can defend myself against the hood kids. It wasn't Earth itself I didn't like, it was what I was doing on Earth I didn't like, and so I sold my UOPWA journeyman's card, mortgaged my pension accrual, and bought a one-way ticket to Venus. Nothing strange about that. What every kid tells himself he's going to do, really. But I did it.

I suppose it would have been all different if I'd had a chance at Real Money. If my father had been Full

Governor instead of a civil-service client. If the dependency benefits had included Unlimited Medicare. If I'd been at the top instead of in the middle, squeezed both ways. It didn't happen that way, so I opted out by the pioneer route and wound up hunting Terry marks at the Spindle.

Everybody has seen pictures of the Spindle, the Colosseum and Niagara Falls. Like everything worth looking at on Venus, the Spindle was a Heechee leftover. Nobody had ever figured out what the Heechee wanted with an underground chamber three hundred meters long and spindle-shaped, but it was there, so we used it; it was the closest thing Venus had to a Times Square or a Camps Elysées. All Terry tourists head for it first. That's where we fleece them.

My airbody-rental business is reasonably legitimate —not counting the fact that there really isn't much worth seeing on Venus that wasn't left there, below the surface, by the Heechee. The other tourist traps in the Spindle are reasonably crooked. Terries don't mind, although they must know they're being taken; they all load up on Heechee prayer fans and doll-heads, and those paperweights of transparent plastic in which a contoured globe of Venus swims in a kind of orange-brown snowstorm of make-believe fly ash, blood-diamonds, and fire-pearls. None of them are worth the price of their mass-charge back to Earth, but to a tourist who can get up the price of passage in the first place I don't suppose that matters.

To people like me, who can't get the price of anything, the tourist traps matter a lot. We live on them. I don't mean we draw our disposable income from them; I mean that they are how we get the price of what to eat and where to sleep, and if we don't have the price we die. There aren't too many ways of earning money on Venus. The ones that might produce Real Money—oh, winning a lottery; striking it rich in the Heechee diggings; blundering into a well-paying job; that kind of thing—are all real long-shots. For bread and butter everybody on Venus depends on Terry tourists, and if we don't milk them dry we've had it.

Of course, there are tourists and tourists. They come in three varieties. The difference between them is celestial mechanics.

There's the quick-and-dirty kind. On Earth, they're just well-to-do; they come every twenty-six months at Hohmann-orbit time, riding the minimum-energy circuit from Earth. Because of the critical times of a Hohmann orbit, they never can stay more than three weeks on Venus. So they come on the guided tours, determined to get the most out of the quarter-million-dollar minimum cabin fare their rich grandparents had given them for a graduation present, or they'd saved up for a second honeymoon, or whatever. The bad thing about them is that they don't have much money, since they'd spent it all on fares. The nice thing about them is that there are a lot of them. While they're on Venus, all the rental rooms are filled. Sometimes they'd have six couples sharing a single partitioned cubicle, two pairs at a time, hot-bedding eight-hour shifts around the clock. Then people like me would hold up in Heechee huts on the surface and rent out our own below-ground rooms, and maybe make enough money to live a few months.

But you couldn't make enough money to live until the next Hohmann-orbit time, so when the Class II tourists came along we cut each other's throats over them.

They were medium-rich. What you might call the poor millionaires: the ones whose annual income was barely in seven figures. They could afford to come in powered orbits, taking a hundred days or so for the run, instead of the long, slow Hohmann drift. The price ran a million dollars and up, so there weren't nearly as many of them; but they came every month or so at the times of reasonably favorable orbital conjunctions. They also had more money to spend. So did the other medium-rich ones who hit us four or five times in a decade, when the ballistics of the planets had sorted themselves out into a low-energy configuration that allowed three planets to come into an orbit that didn't have much higher energy cost than the straight Earth-Venus run. They'd hit us first, if we were lucky, then go on to Mars. If it was the other way around, we got the leavings. The leavings were never very much.

But the very rich—ah, the very rich! They came as they liked, in orbital season or out.

When my tipper on the landing pad reported the *Yuri Gagarin,* under private charter, my money nose began to quiver. It was out of season for everybody except the very rich; the only question on my mind was how many of my competitors would be trying to cut my throat for its passengers while I was cutting theirs.

Airbody rental takes a lot more capital than opening a prayer-fan booth. I'd been lucky in buying my airbody cheap when the fellow I worked for died; I didn't have too many competitors, and a couple of them were U/S for repairs, a couple more had kited off on Heechee diggings of their own.

So, actually, I had the Gagarin's passengers, whoever they were, pretty much to myself. Assuming they could be interested in taking a trip outside the Heechee tunnels.

I had to assume they would be interested, because I needed the money very much. I had this little liver condition, you see. It was getting pretty close to total failure. The way the doctors explained it to me, I had like three choices: I could go back to Earth and linger a while on external prostheses; or I could get up the money for a transplant. Or I could die.

II

The name of the fellow who had chartered the *Gagarin* was Boyce Cochenour. Age, apparently forty. Height, two meters. Ancestry, Irish-American-French.

He was the kind of fellow who was used to command. I watched him come into the Spindle as though it belonged to him and he was getting ready to sell it. He sat down in Sub Vastra's imitation Paris Boulevard-Heechee sidewalk cafe. "Scotch," he said, and Vastra hurried to pour John Begg over super-cooled ice and hand it to him, all crackling with cold and numbing to the lips. "Smoke," he said, and the girl who was traveling with him instantly lit a cigarette and passed it to him. "Crummy looking joint," he said, and Vastra fell all over himself to agree.

I sat down next to them—well, not at the same table, I mean; I didn't even look at them. But I could hear what they said. Vastra didn't look at me, either, but of course he had seen me come in and knew I had my eye on them. But I had to let his number-three wife take my order, because Vastra wasn't going to waste any time on me when he had a charter-ship Terry at his table. "The usual," I said to her, meaning straight-alk in a tumbler of soft drink. "And a copy of your briefing," I added, more softly. Her eyes twinkled at me over her flirtation veil. Cute little vixen. I patted her hand in a friendly way, and left a rolled-up bill in it; then she left.

The Terry was inspecting his surroundings, including me. I looked back at him, polite but distant, and he gave me a sort of quarter-nod and turned back to Subhash Vastra. "Since I'm here," he said, "I might as well go along with whatever action there is. What's to do here?"

Sub grinned widely, like a tall, skinny frog. "Ah, whatever you wish, sah! Entertainment? In our private rooms we have the finest artists of three planets, nautch dancers, music, fine comedians—"

"We've got plenty of that in Cincinnati. I didn't come to Venus for a night club act." He wouldn't have known it, of course, but that was a good move; Sub's private rooms were way down the list of night spots on Venus, and the top of the list wasn't much.

"Of course, sah! Then perhaps you would like to consider a tour?"

"Aw." Cochenour shook his head. "What's the point? Does any of it look any different than the spacepad we came in on, right over our heads?"

Vastra hesitated; I could see him calculating second-order consequences in his head, measuring the chance of the Terry going for a surface tour against what he might get from me as commission. He didn't look my way. Honesty won out—that is, honesty reinforced by a quick appraisal of Cochenour's gullibility. "Not much different, no, sah," he admitted. "All pretty hot and dry on the surface, at least for the next thousand kilometers. But I wasn't thinking of the surface."

"What then?"

"Ah, the Heechee warrens, sah! There are many miles just below this settlement. A guide could be found—"

"Not interested," Cochenour growled. "Not in anything that close."

"Sah?"

"If a guide can lead us through them," Cochenour

134

explained, "that means they've all been explored. Which means they've been looted. What's the fun of that?"

"Of course," said Vastra immediately. "I see what you're driving at, sah." He looked noticeably happier, and I could feel his radar reaching out to make sure I was listening, though he didn't look in my direction at all. "To be sure," he said, "there is always the chance of finding new digs, sah, provided one knows where to look. Am I correct in assuming that this would interest you?"

The third of Vastra's house brought me my drink and a thin powder-faxed slip of paper. "Thirty percent," I whispered to her. "Tell Sub. Only no bargaining, no getting anybody else to bid—" She nodded and winked; she'd been listening too, and she was as sure as I that this Terry was firmly on the hook. It had been my intention to nurse the drink as long as I could, but prosperity loomed before me; I was ready to celebrate; I took a long happy swallow.

But the hook didn't have a barb. Unaccountably the Terry shrugged. "Waste of time, I bet," he grumbled. "I mean, really. If you knew where to look, why wouldn't you have looked there already, right?"

"Ah, mister," cried Subhash Vastra, "but there are hundreds of tunnels not explored! Thousands! And in them, who knows, treasures beyond price!"

Cochenour shook his head. "Skip it;" he said. "Bring us another drink. And see if you can't get the ice *cold* this time."

Somewhat shaken, I put down my drink, half-turned away to hide my hand from the Terries, and looked at the facsimile copy of Sub's report on them to see if it could tell me why Cochenour had lost interest.

It couldn't. It did tell me a lot, though. The girl with Cochenour was named Dorotha Keefer. She had been traveling with him for a couple of years now, this being their first time off Earth; there was no indication of any marriage, or any intention of it, at least on his part. She was in her early twenties—real age, not simulated by drugs and transplants. Cochenour himself was well over ninety.

He did not, of course, look anywhere near that. I'd watched him come over to the table, and he moved lightly and easily, for a big man. His money came from land and petro-foods; according to the synoptic on him, he had been one of the first oil millionaires to switch over from selling oil as fuel for cars and heating plants to food production, growing algae in the crude that came out of his wells and selling the algae in processed form for human consumption. So he'd stopped being a mere millionaire and turned into something much bigger.

And that accounted for the way he looked. He'd been on Full Medical, with extras. The report said his heart was titanium and plastic. His lungs had been transplanted from a twenty-year-old killed in a copter crash. His skin, muscles and fats—not to mention his various glandular systems—were sustained by hormones and cell-builders at what had to be a cost of well over a thousand dollars a day. To judge by the way he stroked the girl sitting next to him, he was getting his money's worth. He looked and acted no more than forty, at most—except perhaps for the look of his pale-blue, diamond-bright, weary and disillusioned eyes.

What a lovely mark! I swallowed the rest of my drink, and nodded to the third for another. There had to be a way to get him to charter my airbody.

All I had to do was find it.

Outside the rail of Vastra's cafe, of course, half the Spindle was thinking exactly the same thoughts. This was the worst of the low season, the Hohmann crowd were still three months in the future; all of us were beginning to run low on money. My liver transplant was just a little extra incentive; of the hundred maze-runners I could see out of the corner of my eye, ninety-nine needed to cut in on this rich tourist's money as much as I did, just for the sake of staying alive.

We couldn't all do it. Two of us, three, maybe even half a dozen could score enough to make a real difference. No more than that. And I had to be one of these few.

I took a deep swallow of my second drink, tipped Vastra's third lavishly—and conspicuously—and turned idly around until I was facing the Terries dead on.

The girl was talking with a knot of souvenir vendors, looking interested and uncertain. "Boyce?" she said over her shoulder.

"Yeah?"

"What's this thing for?"

He bent over the rail and peered. "Looks like a fan," he said.

"Heechee prayer fan, right," cried the dealer; I knew him, Booker Allemang, an old timer in the Spindle. "Found it myself, miss! It'll grant your every wish, letters every day from people reporting miraculous results—"

"Sucker bait," grumbled Cochenour. "Buy it if you want."

"But what does it do?"

He laughed raucously. "What any fan does. It cools you down." And he looked at me, grinning.

I finished my drink, nodded, stood up and walked over to the table. "Welcome to Venus," I said. "May I help you?"

The girl looked at Cochenour for approval before she said, "I thought this was very pretty."

"Very pretty," I agreed. "Are you familiar with the story of the Heechees?"

Cochenour pointed to a chair. I sat and went on. "They built these tunnels about a quarter of a million years ago. They lived here for a couple of centuries, give or take a lot. Then they went away again. They left a lot of junk behind, and some things that weren't junk; among other things they left a lot of these fans. Some local con-man like BeeGee here got the idea of calling them 'prayer fans' and selling them to tourists to make wishes with."

Allemang had been hanging on my every word trying to guess where I was going. "You know it's right," he said.

"But you two are too smart for that kind of come on," I added. "Still, look at the things. They're pretty enough to be worth having even without the story."

"Absolutely!" cried Allemang. "See how this one sparkles, miss! And the black and gray crystal, how nice it looks with your fair hair!"

The girl unfurled the crystalline one. It came rolled like a diploma, only cone-shaped. It took just the slightest pressure of the thumb to keep it open, and it really was very pretty as she waved it gently. Like all the Heechee fans, it weighed only about 10 grams, and its crystalline lattice caught the lights from the luminous Heechee walls, as well as the fluorescents and gas tubes we maze-runners had installed, and tossed them all back in iridescent sparks.

"This fellow's name is Booker Garey Allemang," I said. "He'll sell you the same goods as any of the others, but he won't cheat you as much as most of them."

Cochenour looked at me dourly, then beckoned Sub

Vastra for another round of drinks. "All right," he said. "If we buy, we'll buy from you, Booker Garey Allemang. But not now."

He turned to me. "And what do you want to sell me?"

"Myself and my airbody, if you want to go looking for new tunnels. We're both as good as you can get."

"How much?"

"One million dollars," I said immediately. "All found."

He didn't answer at once, though it gave me some pleasure to notice that the price didn't seem to scare him. He looked as pleasant, or anyway as unangrily bored, as ever. "Drink up," he said, as Vastra and his third served us, and gestured with his glass to the Spindle. "Know what this was for?" he asked.

"You mean why the Heechees built it? No. They were pretty small, so it wasn't for headroom. And it was entirely empty when it was found."

He gazed tolerantly at the busy scene, balconies cut into the sloping sides of the Spindle with eating and drinking places like Vastra's, rows of souvenir booths, most of them empty at this idle season. But there were still a couple of hundred maze-rats around, and the number had been quietly growing all the time Cochenour and the girl had been sitting there.

He said, "It's not much to see, is it? A hole in the ground, and a lot of people trying to take my money away from me."

I shrugged.

He grinned again. "So why did I come, eh? Well, that's a good question, but since you didn't ask it I don't have to answer it. You want a million dollars. Let's see. A hundred K to charter an airbody. A hundred and eighty or so to rent equipment, per week. Ten days minimum, three week a safer guess. Food, supplies, permits, another fifty K. So we're up to close to seven hundred thousand, not counting your own salary and what you give our host here as his cut for not throwing you off the premises. Right, Walthers?"

I had a little difficulty in swallowing the drink I had been holding to my mouth, but I managed to say, "Close enough, Mr. Cochenour." I didn't see any point in telling him that I already owned the equipment, as well as the airbody, although I wouldn't have been surprised to find out that he knew that too.

"You've got a deal, then. And I want to leave as soon as possible, which should be, um, about this time tomorrow."

"Fair enough," I said, and got up, avoiding Sub Vastra's thunderstricken expression. I had some work to do, and a little thinking. He'd caught me off base, which is a bad place to be when you can't afford to make a mistake. I knew he hadn't missed my calling him by name. That was all right; he'd known that I had checked him out immediately. But it was a little surprising that he had known mine.

III

The first thing I had to do was double-check my equipment; the second was go to the local, validate a contract, and settle up with Sub Vastra; the third was see my doctor. The liver hadn't been giving me much trouble for a while, but then I hadn't been drinking grain alcohol for a while.

It took about an hour to make sure that everything we would need for the expedition was i.s., with all the spare parts I might reasonably fear needing. The Quackery was on my way to the union office, so I stopped in there first. It didn't take long. The news was no worse than I had been ready for; Dr. Morius studied the read-out from his instruments carefully. It turned out to be a hundred and fifty dollars' worth of carefully, and expressed the guarded hope that I would survive three weeks away from his office, provided I took all the stuff he gave me and wandered no more than usual from his dietary restrictions. "And when I get back?" I asked.

"About the same, Audee," he said cheerily. "Total collapse in, ah, oh, maybe ninety more days."

He patted his fingertips. "I hear you've got a live one," he added. "Want me to book you for a transplant?"

"How live did you hear he was?" I asked.

"Oh, the price is the same in any case," he told me good-humoredly. "Two hundred K, plus the hospital, anesthesiologist, pre-op psychiatrist, pharmaceuticals—you've already got the figures."

I did, and I knew that with what I might make from Cochenour, plus what I had put away, plus a small loan on the airbody, I could just about meet it. Leaving me broke when it was over but, of course, alive.

"Go ahead," I said. "Three weeks from tomorrow." And I left him looking mildly pleased, like a Burmese hydro-rice man watching another crop being harvested. Dear daddy. Why hadn't he sent me through medical school instead of giving me an education?

It would have been nice if the Heechee had been the same size as human beings, instead of being about forty percent shorter. In the smaller tunnels, like the one that led to the Local 88 office, I had to half-crouch all the way.

The deputy organizer was waiting for me. He had one of the few good jobs that didn't depend on the tourists, or at least not directly. He said, "Subhash Vastra's been on the line. He says you agreed to thirty percent, and besides you forgot to pay your bar bill to the third of his house."

"Admitted, both ways."

"And you owe me a little too, Audee. Three hundred for a powderfax copy of my report on your pigeon. A hundred for validating your contract with Vastra. And if you want guide's papers, sixteen hundred for that."

I gave him my credit card and he checked the total out of my account into the local's. Then I signed and card-stamped the contract he'd drawn up. Vastra's 30% would not be on the whole million-dollar gross, but on my net; even so, he might make as much out of it as I would, at least in liquid cash, because I'd have to pay off all the outstanding balances on equipment and loans. The factors would carry a man until he scored, but then they wanted to get paid. They knew how long it might be until he scored again.

"Thanks, Audee," said the deputy, nodding over the signed contract. "Anything else I can do for you?"

"Not at your prices," I told him.

"Ah, you're putting me on. 'Boyce Cochenour and Dorotha Keefer, Earth-Ohio, traveling *S. V. Yuri Gagarin,* Odessa registry, chartered. No other passengers.' No other passengers," he repeated, quoting from the synoptic report he'd furnished. "Why, you'll be a rich man, Audee, if you work this pigeon right."

"That's more than I ask," I told him. "All I want is to be a living one."

But it wasn't entirely true. I did have some little hope —not much, not enough to talk about, and in fact I'd never said a word about it to anyone—that I might be coming out of this rather better than merely alive.

There was, however, a problem.

See, in the standard guide's contract and airbody leasing terms, I get my money and that's all I get. If we take a mark like Cochenour on a hunt for new Heechee tunnels and he finds something valuable—marks have, you know; not often, but enough to keep them hopeful —then it's his. We just work for him.

On the other hand, I could have gone out by myself any time and prospected; and then anything I found would be all mine.

Obviously, anybody with any sense would go by himself if he thought he was really going to find anything. But in my case, that wasn't such a good idea. If I staked myself to a trip and lost, I hadn't just wasted time and maybe fifty K in supplies and wear and tear. If I lost, I was dead.

I needed what I would make out of Cochenour to stay alive. Whether we found anything interesting or not, my fee would take care of that.

Unfortunately for my peace of mind, I had a notion that I knew where something very interesting might be found; and my problem was that, as long as I had an all-rights contract with Cochenour, I couldn't afford to find it.

The last stop I made was in my sleeping room. Under the bed, keystoned into the rock, was a guaranteed break-proof safe that held some papers I wanted to have in my pocket from then on.

When I came down onto Venus for the first time, it wasn't scenery that interested me. I wanted to make my fortune.

I didn't see much of the surface of Venus then, or for nearly two years after that. You don't see much in the kind of spacecraft that can land on Venus; a 20,000-millibar surface pressure means you need something a little more rugged than the bubble-ships that go to the Moon or Mars or farther out, and there's not much tolerance in the design for putting unnecessary windows into the hull. It didn't matter much, because anywhere except near the poles there's not much you can see. Everything worth seeing on Venus is *in* Venus, and all of it once belonged to the Heechees.

Not that we know much about the Heechees. We don't even rightly know their name—"heechee" is how somebody once wrote down the sound that a fire-pearl makes when you stroke it, and as that's the only sound anybody knows that's connected with them, it got to be a name.

The hesperologists don't know where the Heechees came from, although there are some markings on scraps of stuff that the Heechees used for paper that seem to be a star chart—faded, incomplete, pretty much unrecognizable; if we know the exact position of every star in the galaxy 250,000 years ago, we might be able to locate them from that, I suppose. Assuming they came from this galaxy. There are no traces of them anywhere else in the solar system. except maybe in Phobos; the experts still fight about whether the honeycomb cells inside the Martian moon are natural or artifacts, and if they're artifacts they're no doubt Heechee. But they don't look much like ours.

I wonder sometimes what they wanted. Escaping a dying planet? Political refugees? Tourists that had a breakdown between somewhere and somewhere, and hung around just long enough to make whatever, they had to make to get themselves going again? I used to think that they'd maybe come by to watch human beings evolving on Earth, sort of stepfathers beaming over the growing young race; but we couldn't have been much to watch at that time, halfway between the Australopithecines and the Cro-Magnards.

But, though they packed up nearly everything when they left, leaving behind only empty tunnels and chambers, there were a few scraps here and there that either weren't worth taking along or were overlooked: all those "prayer fans", enough empty containers of one kind or another to look like a picnic ground at the end of a hard summer, some trinkets and trifles. I guess the best known of the "trifles" is the anisokinetic punch, the carbon crystal that transmits a blow at a ninety-degree angle; that made somebody a few billion just by being lucky enough to find one, and smart enough to analyze and duplicate it. But all we've ever found is junk. There must have been good stuff worth a million times as much as those sweepings.

Did they take all the good stuff with them?

Nobody knew. I didn't know, either, but I did think I knew something that had a bearing on it.

I thought I knew where the last Heechee ship had taken off from; and it wasn't near any of the explored diggings.

I didn't kid myself. I knew that wasn't a guarantee of anything.

But it was something to go on. *Maybe* when that last ship left they were getting impatient, and maybe not as thorough in cleaning up behind themselves.

And that was what being on Venus was all about. What other possible reason was there for being there? The life of a maze-rat was marginal at best. It took fifty thousand a year to stay alive. If you had less than that you couldn't pay air tax, capitation tax, water assessment, or even a subsistence-level bill for food. If you wanted to eat meat more than once a week, and demanded a cubicle of your own to sleep in, it cost more than that.

Guide's papers cost a week's life; when any of us bought them, we were gambling that week's cost-of-living against the chance of a big enough strike, either from the Terry tourists or from what we might find, to make it possible to get back to Earth—where no one starved, no one died for lack of air, no one was thrust out into the high-pressure incinerator that was Venus's atmosphere. Not *just* to get back to Earth. To get back in the style every maze-rat had set himself as a goal when he headed sunward in the first place: with money enough to live the full life of a human being on Full Medical.

That was what I wanted. The big score.

IV

Not by accident, the last thing I did that night was to visit the Hall of Discoveries.

The third of Vastra's house winked at me over her flirtation veil and turned to her companion, who looked around and nodded.

I joined them. "Hello, Mr. Walthers," she said.

"I thought I might find you here," I said, which was no more than the truth, since Vastra's third had promised to guide her this way. I didn't know what to call her. "Miss Keefer" was accurate, "Mrs. Cochenour" was diplomatic; I got around it by saying, "Since we'll be seeing a lot of each other, how about getting on to first names?"

"Audee, is it?"

I gave her a twelve-tooth smile. "Swede on my mother's side, old Texan on my father's. Name's been in his family a long time, I guess."

The Hall of Discoveries is meant to get Terry prospects hotted up; there's a little of everything in it, from charts of the worked diggings and a full-scale Mercator map of Venus to samples of all the principal finds. I showed her the copy of the anisokinetic punch, and the original solid-state piezophone that had made its discoverer almost as permanently rich as the guy who found the punch. There were about a dozen fire-pearls, quarter-inch jobbies, behind armor glass, on cushions, blazing away with their cold milky light.

"They're pretty," she said. "But why all the protection? I saw bigger ones lying on a counter in the Spindle without anybody even watching them."

"That's a little different, Dorotha," I told her. "These are real."

She laughed out loud. It was a very nice laugh. No girl looks beautiful when she's laughing hard, and girls who worry about looking beautiful don't do it. Dorotha Keefer looked like a healthy, pretty girl having a good time, which when you come down to it is about the best way for a girl to look.

She did not, however, look good enough to come between me and a new liver, so I took my mind off that aspect of her and put it on business. "The little red marbles over there are blood-diamonds," I told her. "They're radioactive and stay warm. Which is one way you can tell the real one from a fake: Anything over about three centimeters is a fake. A real one that big generates too much heat—square-cube law, you know —and melts."

"So the ones your friend was trying to sell me—"

"—are fakes. Right."

She nodded, still smiling. "What about what you were trying to sell us, Audee? Real or fake?"

The third of Vastra's house had discreetly vanished, and there was nobody else in the Hall of Discoveries but me and the girl. I took a deep breath and told her the truth. Not the whole truth, maybe; but nothing but the truth.

"All this stuff," I said, "is what came out of a hundred years of digging. And it's not much. The punch, the piezophone, and two or three other gadgets that we can make work; a few busted pieces of things that they're still studying; and some trinkets. That's all."

She said, "That's the way I heard it. And one more thing. None of the discovery dates on these things is less than fifty years old."

She was smart and better informed than I had expected. "And the conclusion," I agreed, "is that the planet has been mined dry. You're right, on the evidence. The first diggers found everything there was to be found . . . so far."

"You think there's more?"

"I *hope* there's more. Look. Item. The tunnels. You see they're all alike—the blue walls, perfectly smooth; the light coming from them that never varies; the hardness. How do you suppose they were made?"

"Why, I don't know—"

"Neither do I. Or anybody else. But every Heechee tunnel is the same, and if you dig into them from the outside you find the basic substrate rock, then a boundary layer that's sort of half wall-stuff and half substrate, then the wall. Conclusion: The Heechees didn't dig the tunnels and then line them, they had something that crawled around underground like an earthworm, leaving these tunnels behind. And one other thing: They overdug. That's to say they dug tunnels they didn't need, lots of them, going nowhere, never used for anything. Does that suggest anything to you?"

"It must have been cheap and easy?" she guessed.

I nodded. "So it was probably a machine, and there really ought to be at least one of them, somewhere on this planet, to find. Next item. The air: They breathed oxygen like we do, and they must have got it from somewhere. Where?"

"Why, there's oxygen in the atmosphere—"

"Sure. About a half of one percent. And better

than 95 percent carbon dioxide; and somehow they managed to get that half of one percent out of the mixture, cheaply and easily—remember those extra tunnels they filled!—along with enough nitrogen or some other inert gas—and they're present in only trace amounts—to make a breathing mixture. How? Why, I don't know, but if there's a machine that did it, I'd like to find that machine. Next item: Aircraft. The Heechee flew around the surface of Venus at will."

"So do you, Audee! Aren't you a pilot?"

"Sure, but look at what it takes. Surface temperature of two-seventy C, and not enough oxygen to keep a cigarette going. So my airbody has two fuel tanks, one for hydrocarbons, one for oxidants. And—did you ever hear of a fellow named Carnot?"

"Old-time scientist, was he? The Carnot cycle?"

"Right again." That was the third time she'd surprised me, I noted cautiously. "The Carnot efficiency of an engine is expressed by its maximum temperature—the heat of combustion, let's say—over the temperature of its exhaust. Well, but the temperature of the exhaust can't be less than the temperature of what it flows into —otherwise you're not running an engine, you're running a refrigerator. And you've got that two-seventy ambient air temperature; so you have basically a lousy engine. *Any* heat engine on Venus is lousy. Did you ever wonder why there are so few airbodies around? I don't mind; it helps to have something close to a monopoly. But the reason is they're so damn expensive to run."

"And the Heechees did it better?"

"I *think* they did."

She laughed again, unexpectedly and once more very attractively. "Why, you poor fellow," she said in good humor, "you're hooked on the stuff you sell, aren't you?

149

You think that some day you're going to find the mother tunnel and pick up all this stuff."

Well, I wasn't too pleased with the way things were going; I'd arranged with Vastra's third to bring the girl here, away from her boy friend, so I could pick her brains in private. It hadn't worked out that way. The way it was working out, she was making me aware of her as a person, which was a bad development in itself, and worse than that, making me take a good look at myself.

I said after a minute, "You may be right. But I'm sure going to give it a good try."

"You're angry, aren't you?"

"No," I said, lying, "but maybe a little tired. And we've got a long trip tomorrow, so I'd better take you home. Miss Keefer."

V

My airbody lay by the spacepad and was reached the same way the spacepad was reached. Elevator to the surface lock, a tractor-cab to carry us across the dry, tortured surface of Venus, peeling under the three hundred kilometer an hour wind. Normally I kept it under a foam housing, of course. You don't leave anything free and exposed on the surface of Venus if you want to keep it intact, not even if it's made of chrome steel. I'd had the foam stripped free when I checked it out and loaded supplies that morning. Now it was ready. I could see it from the bull's-eye ports of the crawler, through the green-yellow murk outside. Cochenour and the girl could have seen it too, if they'd known where to look, but they might not have recognized it.

Cochenour screamed in my ear, "You and Dorrie have a fight?"

"No fight," I screamed back.

"Don't care if you did. You don't have to like each other, just do what I want you to do." He was silent a moment, resting his throat. "Jesus. What a wind."

"Zephyr," I told him. I didn't say any more, he would find out for himself. The area around the space-pad is a sort of natural calm area, by Venusian standards. Orographic lift throws the meanest winds up over the pad and all we get is a sort of confused back eddy. The good part is that taking off and landing are relatively easy. The bad part is that some of the heavy metal compounds in the atmosphere settle out on the pad. What passes for air on Venus has layers of red mercuric sulfide and mercurous chloride in the lower reaches, and when you get above them to those pretty fluffy clouds you find some of them are hydrochloric and hydrofluoric acid.

But there are tricks to that, too. Navigation over Venus is 3-D. It's easy enough to proceed from point to point; your transponders will link you to the radio-range and map your position continuously onto the charts. What's hard is to find the right altitude, and that's why my airbody and I were worth a million dollars to Cochenour.

We were at the airbody, and the telescoping snout from the crawler was poking out to its lock. Cochenour was staring out the bull's eye. "No wings!" he shouted, as though I was cheating him.

"No sails or snow chains, either," I shouted back. "Get aboard if you want to talk! It's easier in the airbody."

We climbed through the little snout, I unlocked the entrance, and we got aboard without much trouble.

We didn't even have the kind of trouble that I might have made myself. You see, an airbody is a big thing on Venus. I was damn lucky to have been able to acquire it and, well, I won't beat around the bush, you could say I loved it. Mine could have held ten people, without equipment. With what Sub Vastra's purchasing department had sold us and Local 88 had certified as essential aboard, it was crowded with just the three of us. I was prepared for sarcasm, at least. But Cochenour merely looked around long enough to find the best bunk, strode over to it and declared it his. The girl was a good sport, and there I was, left with my glands all charged up for an argument and no argument.

It was a lot quieter inside the airbody. You could hear the noise of the wind right enough, but it was only annoying. I passed out earplugs, and with them in place the noise was hardly even annoying.

"Sit down and strap up," I ordered, and when they were stowed away I took off.

At twenty thousand millibars wings aren't just useless, they're poison. My airbody had all the lift it needed built into the seashell-shaped hull. I fed the double fuels into the thermojets, we bounced across the reasonably flat ground around the spacepad (it was bulldozed once a week, which is how come it stayed reasonably flat) and we were zooming off into the wild yellow-green yonder, a moment later the wild brown-gray yonder, after a run of no more than fifty meters.

Cochenour had fastened his harness loosely for comfort. I enjoyed hearing him yell as he was thrown about. It didn't last. At the thousand-meter level I found Venus's semi-permanent atmospheric inversion, and the turbulence dropped to where I could take off my belt and stand.

I took the plugs out of my ears and motioned to Cochenour and the girl to do the same.

He was rubbing his head where he'd bounced into an overhead chart rack, but grinning a little. "Pretty

152

exciting," he admitted, fumbling in his pocket. Then he remembered to ask. "Is it all right if I smoke?"

"They're your lungs."

He grinned more widely. "They are now," he agreed, and lit up. "Say. Why didn't you give us those plugs while we were in the tractor?"

There is, as you might say, a tide in the affairs of guides, where you either let them flood you with questions and spend the whole time explaining what that funny little dial means or you go on to do your work and make your fortune. What it came down to was, was I going to come out of this liking Cochenour and his girl friend or not?

If I was, I should try to be civil to them. More than civil. Living, the three of us, for three weeks in a space about as big as an apartment kitchenette meant everybody would have to work real hard at being nice to everybody else, and as I was the one who was being paid to be nice, I should be the one to set an example. On the other hand, the Cochenours of the worlds are sometimes just not likeable. If that was going to be the case, the less talk the better; I should slide questions like that off with something like "I forgot."

But he hadn't actually been unpleasant, and the girl friend had actually tried to be friendly. I said, "Well, that's an interesting thing. You see, you hear by differences in pressure. While we were taking off the plugs filtered out part of the sound—the pressure waves—but when I yelled at you to belt up, the plugs passed the overpressure of my voice, and you understood it. However, there's a limit. Past about a hundred and twenty decibels—that's a unit of sound—"

Cochenour growled, "I know what a decibel is."

"Right. Past a hundred and twenty the eardrum just doesn't respond any more. So in the crawler it was

153

too loud; with the plugs, you wouldn't have heard anything."

Dorotha had been listening while she repaired her eye makeup. "What was to hear?"

"Oh," I said, "nothing, really. Except, well—" Then I voted to think of them as friends, at least for the time being. "Except in the case of an accident. If we'd had a gust, you know, that crawler could have flipped right over. Or sometimes solid objects come flying over the hills and into you before you know it. Or—"

She was shaking her head. "I understand. Lovely place we're visiting, Boyce."

"Yeah. Look," he said. "Who's flying this thing?"

I got up and activated the virtual globe. "That's what I was just coming to. Right now it's on autopilot, heading in the general direction of this quadrant down here. We have to pick out a specific destination."

"That's Venus?" the girl asked. "It doesn't look like much."

"Those lines are just radio-range markers; you won't see them looking out the window. Venus doesn't have any oceans, and it isn't cut up into nations, so making a map of it isn't quite like what you'd expect on Earth. That bright spot is us. Now look." I overlaid the radio-range grid and the contour colors with mascon markings. "Those blobby circles are mascons. You know what a mascon is?"

"A concentration of mass. A lump of heavy stuff," offered the girl.

"Fine. Now look at the known Heechee digs." I phased them in as golden patterns.

"They're all in the mascons," Dorotha said at once. Cochenour gave her a look of tolerant approval.

"Not all. Look over here; this little one isn't, and this one. But damn near all. Why? I don't know. Nobody knows. The mass concentrations are mostly older,

denser rock—basalt and so on—and maybe the Heechee found it easier to dig in. Or maybe they just liked
it." In my correspondence with Professor Hegramet
back on Earth, in the days when I didn't have a dying
liver in my gut and took an interest in abstract knowledge, we had kicked around the possibility that the
Heechee digging machines would only work in dense
rock, or rock of a certain chemical composition.
But I wasn't prepared to discuss that with them.

"See over here, where we are now"—I rotated the
virtual globe slightly by turning a dial—"that's the big
digging we just came out of. You can see the shape of
the Spindle. It's a common shape, by the way. You
can see it in some of the others if you look, and there
are digs where it doesn't show on these tracings but it's
there if you're on the spot. That particular mascon
where the Spindle is is called Serendip; it was discovered
by accident by a hesperological—"

"Hesperological?"

"—a geological team operating on Venus, which
makes it a hesperological team. They were drilling out
core samples and hit the Heechee digs. Now these
other digs in the northern high-latitudes you see are all
in one bunch of associated mascons. They connect
through interventions of less dense rock, but only
where absolutely necessary."

Cochenour said sharply, "They're north and we're
going south. Why?"

It was interesting that he could read the navigation instruments, but I didn't say so. I only said,
"They're no good. They've been probed."

"They look even bigger than the Spindle."

"Hell of a lot bigger, right. But there's nothing much
in them, or anyway not much chance that anything in
them is in good enough shape to bother with. Subsurface
fluids filled them up a hundred thousand years ago,

maybe more. A lot of good men have gone broke trying to pump and excavate them, without finding anything. Ask me. I was one of them."

"I didn't know there was any liquid water on Venus or under it," Cochenour objected.

"I didn't say water, did I? But as a matter of fact some of it was, or anyway a sort of oozy mud. Apparently water cooks out of the rocks and has a transit time to the surface of some thousands of years before it seeps out, boils off, and cracks to hydrogen and oxygen and gets lost. In case you didn't know it, there's some under the Spindle. It's what you were drinking, and what you were breathing."

The girl said, "Boyce, this is all very interesting, but I'm hot and dirty. Can I change the subject for a minute?"

Cochenour barked; it wasn't really a laugh. "Subliminal prompting, Walthers, you agree? And a little old-fashioned prudery, too, I expect. What she really wants to do is go to the bathroom."

Given a little encouragement from the girl, I would have been mildly embarrassed for her, but she only said, "If we're going to live in this thing for three weeks, I'd like to know what it offers."

I said, "Certainly, Miss Keefer."

"Dorotha. Dorrie, if you like it better."

"Sure, Dorrie. Well, you see what we've got. Five bunks; they partition to sleep ten if wanted, but we don't want. Two shower stalls. They don't look big enough to soap yourself in, but they are if you work at it. Three chemical toilets. Kitchen over there—well. Pick the bunk you like, Dorrie. There's a screen arrangement that comes down when you want it for changing clothes and so on, or just if you don't want to look at the rest of us for a while."

Cochenour said, "Go on, Dorrie, do what you want

to do. I want Walthers to show me how to fly this thing anyway."

It wasn't a bad start. I've had some real traumatic times, parties that came aboard drunk and steadily got drunker, couples that fought every waking minute and got together only to hassle me. This one didn't look bad at all, apart from the fact that it was going to save my life for me.

There's not much to flying an airbody, at least as far as making it move the way you want it to is concerned. In Venus's atmosphere there's lift to spare. You don't worry about things like stalling out; and anyway the autonomic controls do most of your thinking for you.

Cochenour learned fast. It turned out he had flown everything that moved on Earth and operated one-man submersibles as well. He understood as soon as I mentioned it to him that the hard part of pilotage was selecting the right flying level and anticipating when you'd have to change it, but he also understood that he wasn't going to learn that in one day. Or even in three weeks. "What the hell, Walthers," he said cheerfully enough. "At least I can make it go where I have to, in case you get caught in a tunnel or shot by a jealous husband."

I gave him the smile his pleasantry was worth, which wasn't much. "The other thing I can do," he said, "is cook. Unless you're really good at it? No, I thought not. Well, I paid too much for this stomach to fill it with hash, so I'll make the meals. That's a little skill Dorrie never got around to learning. Same with her grandmother. Most beautiful woman in the world, but had the idea that was all there was to it."

I put that aside to sort out later; he was full of little unexpected things, this 90-year-old young athlete. He said, "All right, now while Dorrie's using up all the water in the shower——"

"Not to worry; it all recycles."

"Anyway. While she's cleaning up, finish your little lecture on where we're going."

"Right." I spun the virtual globe a little. The bright spot that was us had moved a dozen degrees already. "See that cluster where our track intersects those grid marks?"

"Yeah. Five big mascons close together, and no diggings indicated. Is that where we're going?"

"In a general sense, yes."

"Why in a general sense?"

"Well," I said, "there's one little thing I didn't tell you. I'm assuming you won't jump salty over it, because then I'll have to get salty too and tell you you should have taken the trouble to learn more about Venus before you decided to explore it."

He studied me appraisingly for a moment. Dorrie came quietly out of the shower in a long robe, her hair in a towel, and stood near him, watching. "It depends on what you didn't tell me," he said.

"There's a no-trespassing sign on most of those mascons," I said. I activated the pilotage chart overlay, and bright cherry-red warning lines sprang up all around the cluster.

"That's the south polar security area," I said. "That's where the Defense boys keep the missile range and the biggest part of their weapons development areas. And we're not allowed to enter."

He said harshly, "But there's only a little piece of one mascon that isn't off limits."

"And that's where we're going," I said.

VI

For a man more than ninety years old, Boyce Cochenour was spry. I don't mean just healthy looking. Full Medical will do that for you, because you just replace whatever wears out or begins to look shopworn and tatty. You cannot, however, very well replace the brain, so what you usually see in the very rich old ones is a bronzed, strong body that shakes and hesitates and drops things and stumbles. About that Cochenour had been very lucky.

He was going to be wearing company for three weeks. He'd insisted I show him how to pilot the airbody. When I decided to use a little flight time to give the cooling system a somewhat premature thousand-hour check, he helped me pull the covers, check the refrigerant levels and clean the filters. Then he decided to cook us lunch.

The girl took over as my helper while I restowed some of the supplies to get the autosonic probes out. At the steady noise level of the inside of an airbody our normal conversational voices wouldn't carry to Cochenour, less than three meters away, and I thought of pumping her about him. I decided against it. What I didn't know was just curiosity. I knew he was paying me the price of a new liver already. I didn't need to know what he and the girl thought about when they thought about each other.

So our conversation was along the lines of how the probes would fire charges and time the echoes, and what the chances were of finding something really good ("Well, what are the chances of winning a sweepstakes? Bad for any individual who buys a ticket—but there's always one winner somewhere!"), and what had made me come to Venus in the first place. I mentioned my father's name, but she'd never heard of him. Too young, for one thing, no doubt. And she was born and bred in Southern Ohio, where Cochenour had worked as a kid and to which he'd returned as a billionaire. He'd been building a new processing center there and it had been a lot of headaches—trouble with the unions, trouble with the banks, trouble, bad trouble, with the government—so he'd decided to take a few months off and loaf. I looked over to where he was stirring up a sauce and said, "He loafs harder than anybody else I ever saw."

"He's a work addict. I imagine that's how he got rich in the first place." The airbody lurched, and I dropped everything to jump for the controls. I heard Cochenour howl behind me, but I was busy locating the right transit level. By the time I had climbed a thousand meters and reset the autopilot, he was rubbing his wrist and glowering at me.

"Sorry," I said.

He said dourly, "I don't mind your scalding the skin off my arm, I can always buy more skin, but you nearly made me spill the gravy."

I checked the virtual globe. The bright marker was two-thirds of the way to our destination. "Is it about ready?" I asked. "We'll be there in an hour."

For the first time he looked startled. "So soon? I thought you said this thing was subsonic."

"I did. You're on Venus, Mr. Cochenour. At this level the speed of sound is maybe five thousand kilometers an hour."

He looked thoughtful, but all he said was, "Well, we can eat any minute." Later he said, while we were finishing up, "I think maybe I don't know as much about this planet as I might. If you want to give us the usual guide's lecture, we'll listen."

I said, "Well, you pretty much know the outlines.

160

Say, you're a great cook, Mr. Cochenour. I packed all these provisions, but I don't even know what this is I'm eating."

"If you come to my office in Cincinnati," he said, "you can ask for Mr. Cochenour, but while we're living in each other's armpits you might as well call me Boyce. And if you like it, why aren't you eating it?"

The answer was, because it might kill me, but I didn't want to get into a discussion that might lead to why I needed his fee so badly. I said, "Doctor's orders, have to lay off the fats pretty much for a while. I think he thinks I'm putting on too much weight."

Cochenour looked at me appraisingly, but only said, "The lecture?"

"Well, let's start with the most important part," I said, carefully pouring coffee. "While we're in the air-body you can do what you like, walk around, eat, drink, smoke if you got 'em, whatever. The cooling system is built for more than three times as many people, plus their cooking and appliance loads, with a safety factor of two. Air and water, more than we'd need for two months. Fuel, enough for three round trips and some maneuvering. If anything went wrong we'd yell for help and somebody would come and get us in a couple of hours at most—probably it would be the Defense boys, and they have *super*sonic bodies. The worst thing would be if the hull breached and the whole Venusian atmosphere tried to come in. If it happened fast we'd be dead. It never happens fast, though. We'd have time to get in the suits, and we can live in them for thirty hours. Long before that we'd be picked up."

"Assuming, of course, that nothing went wrong with the radio at the same time," said Cochenour.

"Right. You can get killed anywhere, if enough accidents happen at once."

He poured himself another cup of coffee, tipped a little brandy into it and said, "Go on."

"Well, outside the airbody it's a little more tricky. You've only got the suit, and its useful life, as I say, is only thirty hours. It's a question of refrigeration. You can carry all the air and water you want, and you don't have to worry about food, but it takes a lot of compact energy to get rid of the diffuse energy all around you. It takes fuel for the cooling systems, and when that's gone you better be back in the airbody. Heat isn't the worst way to die. You pass out before you begin to hurt. But the end result is you're dead.

"The other thing is, you want to check your suit every time you put it on. Pressure it up and watch the gauge for leaks. I'll check it too, but *don't rely on me*. It's your life. And the faceplates are pretty strong; you can drive nails with them without breaking them, but they can be broken if hit hard enough against a hard enough surface. That way you're dead too."

Dorrie said quietly, "One question. Have you ever lost a tourist?"

"No." But then I added, "Others have. Five or six get killed every year."

"I don't mind odds like that," said Cochenour. "Actually, that wasn't the lecture I was asking for, Audee. I mean, I certainly want to hear how to stay alive, but I assume you would have told us all this before we left the ship anyway. What I really wanted to know was how come you picked this particular mascon to prospect."

This old geezer with the muscle-beach body was beginning to bother me. He had a disturbing habit of asking the questions I didn't want to answer. There was a reason why I had picked this site; it had to do with about five years of study, a lot of digging, and about a quarter of a million dollars' worth of correspondence, at space-mail rates, with people like Professor Hegramet back on Earth.

But I didn't want to tell him all of my reasons. There were about a dozen sites that I really wanted to explore. If this happened to be one of the payoff places, he would come out of it richer than I would—that's what the contracts you sign say: 40% to the charterer, 25% to the guide, the rest to the government—and that should be enough for him. If it happened not to pay off, I didn't want him taking some other guide to one of the others I'd marked.

So I only said, "Call it an informed guess. I promised you a good shot at a tunnel that's never been opened, and I hope to keep my promise. And now let's get the food put away; we're within ten minutes of where we're going."

With everything strapped down and ourselves belted up, we dropped out of the relatively calm layers into the big winds again.

We were over the big south-central massif, about the same elevation as the lands surrounding the Spindle. That's the elevation where most of the action is on Venus. Down in the lowlands and the deep rift valleys the pressures run fifty thousand millibars and up. My airbody wouldn't take any of that for very long, and neither would anybody else's, except for a few of the special research and military types. Fortunately, the Heechee didn't care for the lowlands either. Nothing of theirs has ever been located much below twenty-bar. Doesn't mean it isn't there, of course.

Anyway, I verified our position on the virtual globe and on the detail charts, and deployed the autosonic probes. The winds threw them all over the place as soon as they dropped free. It doesn't much matter where they go, within broad limits, which is a good thing. They dropped like javelins at first, then flew around like straws until the little rockets cut in and the ground-seeking controls fired them to the ground.

Every one embedded itself properly. You aren't always that lucky, so it was a good start.

I verified their position on the detail charts; it was close enough to an equilateral triangle, which is about how you want them. Then I opened the scanning range and began circling around.

"Now what?" bellowed Cochenour. I noticed the girl had put the earplugs back, but he wasn't willing to miss a thing.

"Now we wait for the probes to feel around for Heechee tunnels. It'll take a couple of hours." While I was talking I brought the airbody down through the surface layers. Now we were being thrown around. The buffeting got pretty bad, and so did the noise.

But I found what I was looking for, a surface formation like a blind arroyo, and tucked us into it with only one or two bad moments. Cochenour was watching very carefully, and I grinned to myself. That was where pilotage counted, not en route or at the prepared pads around the Spindle. When he could do that he could get along without somebody like me.

Our position looked all right, so I fired four hold-downs, tethered stakes with explosive heads that opened out in the ground. I winched them tight and all of them held.

That was also a good sign. Reasonably pleased with myself, I opened the belt catches and stood up. "We're here for at least a day or two," I said. "More if we're lucky. How did you like the ride?"

The girl was taking the earplugs out, now that the protecting walls of the arroyo had cut the thundering down to a mere constant scream. "I'm glad I don't get airsick," she said.

Cochenour was thinking, not talking. He was studying the control board while he lit another cigarette.

Dorotha said, "One question, Audee. Why couldn't we stay up where it's quieter?"

"Fuel. I carry about thirty hours, full thrust, but that's it. Is the noise bothering you?"

She made a face.

"You'll get used to it. It's like living next to a spaceport. At first you wonder how anybody stands the noise for a single hour. After you've been there a week you miss it if it stops."

She moved over to the bull's-eye and gazed pensively out at the landscape. We'd crossed into the night portion, and there wasn't much to see but dust and small objects whirling through our external light beams. "It's that first week that I'm worried about," she said.

I flicked on the probe read-out. The little percussive heads were firing their slap-charges and measuring each other's sounds, but it was too early to see anything. The screen was barely beginning to build up a shadowy pattern, more holes than detail.

Cochenour finally spoke. "How long until you can make some sense out of that?" he demanded. Another point: He didn't ask what it was.

"Depends on how close and how big anything is. You can make a guess in an hour or so, but I like all the data I can get. Six or eight hours, I'd say. There's no hurry."

He growled, "*I'm* in a hurry, Walthers. Keep that in mind."

The girl cut in. "What should we do, Audee? Play three-handed bridge?"

"Whatever you want, but I'd advise some sleep. I've got pills if you want them. If we do find anything— and remember, if we hit on the first try it's just hundred-to-one luck—we'll want to be wide awake for a while."

"All right," said Dorotha, reaching out for the spansules, but Cochenour demanded:

"What about you?"

"Pretty soon. I'm waiting for something." He didn't ask what. Probably, I thought, because he already knew. I decided that when I did hit my bunk I wouldn't take a sleepy pill right away. This Cochenour was not only the richest tourist I had ever guided, he was one of the best informed, and I wanted to think about that for a while.

What I was waiting for took almost an hour to come. The boys were getting a little sloppy; they should have been after us before this.

The radio buzzed and then blared: "Unidentified vessel at one three five, zero seven, four eight and seven two, five one, five four! Please identify yourself and state your purpose!"

Cochenour looked up inquiringly from his gin game with the girl. I smiled reassuringly. "As long as they're saying 'please' there's no problem," I told him, and opened the transmitter.

"This is Pilot Audee Walthers, airbody Poppa Tare Nine One, out of the Spindle. We are licensed and have filed approved flight plans. I have two Terry tourists aboard, purpose recreational exploration."

"Acknowledge. Please wait," blared the radio. The military always broadcasts at maximum gain. Hangover from drill-sergeant days, no doubt.

I turned off the microphone and told my passengers, "They're checking our flight plan. Not to worry about."

In a moment the Defense communicator came back, loud as ever. "You are eleven point four kilometers bearing one eight three degrees from terminator of a restricted area. Proceed with caution. Under Military Regulations One Seven and One Eight, Sections—"

I cut in, "I know the drill. I have my guide's license and have explained the restrictions to the passengers."

"Acknowledged," blared the radio. "We will keep you under surveillance. If you observe vessels or parties on the surface, they are our perimeter teams. Do not interfere with them in any way. Respond at once to any request for identification or information." The carrier buzz cut off.

Cochenour said, "They act nervous."

"No. They're used to seeing us around. They've got nothing else to do, that's all."

Dorrie said hesitantly, "Audee, you told them you'd explained the restrictions to us. I don't remember that part."

"Oh, I explained them all right. We stay out of the restricted area, because if we don't they'll start shooting. That is the Whole of the Law."

VII

I set a wake-up for four hours, and the others heard me moving around and got up too. Dorrie fetched us coffee from the warmer, and we stood drinking it and looking at the patterns the computer had traced.

I took several minutes to study them, although it was clear enough at first look. There were eight major anomalies that could have been Heechee warrens. One was almost right outside our door. We wouldn't even have to move the airbody to dig for it.

I showed them the anomalies, one by one. Cochenour just looked at them thoughtfully. Dorotha asked after a moment, "You mean all of these are unexplored tunnels?"

"No. Wish they were. But, one: Any or all of them could have been explored by someone who didn't go to the trouble of recording it. Two: They don't have to be tunnels. They might be fracture faults, or dikes, or little rivers of some kind of molten material that ran out of somewhere and hardened and got covered over a billion years ago. The only thing we know for sure so far is that there probably aren't any unexplored tunnels in this area *except* in those eight places."

"So what do we do?"

"We dig. And then we see what we've got."

Cochenour said, "Where do we dig?"

I pointed right next to the bright delta of our airbody. "Right here."

"Because it's the best bet?"

"Well, not necessarily." I considered what to tell him, and decided the truth was the best. "There are three that look like better bets than the others—here, I'll mark them." I keyed the chart controls, and the best looking traces immediately displayed letters: A, B and C. "A runs right under the arroyo here, so we'll dig it first."

"Those three because they're the brightest?"

I nodded, somewhat annoyed at his quickness, although it was obvious enough.

"But C over here is the brightest of the lot. Why don't we dig that first?"

I chose my words carefully. "Because we'd have to move the airbody. And because it's on the outside perimeter of the survey area; that means the results aren't as reliable as they are for this one right under us. But those aren't the most important reasons. The most important reason is that C is on the edge of the line our itchy-fingered friends are telling us to stay away from."

Cochenour laughed incredulously. "You mean you're telling me that if you find a real untouched Heechee tunnel you'll stay out of it just because some soldier tells you it's a no-no?"

I said, "The problem doesn't arise just yet; we have seven anomalies to look at that are legal. Also, the military will be checking us from time to time, particularly in the next day or two."

Cochenour insisted, "All right, suppose we check them and find nothing. What do we do then?"

I shook my head. "I never borrow trouble. Let's check the legal ones."

"But suppose."

"Damn it, Boyce! How do I know?"

He gave it up then, but winked at Dorrie and chuckled. "What did I tell you, honey? He's a bigger bandit than I am."

For the next couple of hours we didn't have much time to talk about theoretical possibilities, because we were too busy with concrete facts.

The biggest fact was an awful lot of hot high-speed gas that we had to keep from killing us. My own hot-suit was custom made, of course, and only needed the fittings and tanks to be checked. Boyce and the girl had rental units. They'd paid top dollar for them, and they were good, but good isn't perfect. I had them in and out of them a dozen times, checking the fit and varying tensions until they were as right as I could get them. There's a lot of heat and pressure to keep out when you go about the surface of Venus. The suits were laminated twelve-ply, with nine degrees of freedom at the essential joints. They wouldn't fail; that wasn't what I was worried about. What I was worried about was comfort, because a very small itch or rub can get serious when there's no way to stop it.

But finally they were good enough for a first trial, and we all huddled in the lock and exited onto the surface of Venus.

We were still darkside, but there's so much scatter

from the sun that it doesn't get really dark more than a quarter of the time. I let them practice walking around the airbody, leaning into the wind, bracing themselves against the hold-downs and the side of the ship, while I got ready to dig.

I hauled out our first instant igloo, dragged it into position, and ignited it. As it smoldered it puffed up like the children's toy that used to be called a Pharaoh's Serpent, producing a light, tough ash that grew up around the digging site and joined in a seamless dome at the top. I'd already emplaced the digging torch and the crawl-through lock; as the ash grew I manhandled the lock to get a close union, and got a perfect join first time.

Dorrie and Cochenour stayed out of the way when they caught sight of my waving arm, but hung together, watching through their triple-vision plugs. I keyed on the radio. "You want to come in and watch me start it up?" I shouted.

Inside the helmets, they both nodded their heads. "Come on, then," I yelled, and wiggled through the crawl lock. I signed for them to leave it open as they followed me in.

With the three of us and the digging equipment in it, the igloo was even more crowded than the airbody. They backed away as far as they could get, bent against the arc of the igloo wall, while I started up the augers, checked they were vertical, and watched the first castings spiral out.

The foam igloo absorbs more sound than it reflects. Even so, the din inside the igloo was a lot worse than in the howling winds outside. When I thought they'd seen enough to satisfy them for the moment, I waved them out of the crawl-through, followed, sealed it behind us, and led them back into the airbody.

"So far, so good," I said, twisting off the helmet and

170

loosening the suit. "We've got about forty meters to go, I think. Might as well wait in here as out there."

"How long is that?"

"Maybe an hour. You can do what you like; what I'm going to do is take a shower. Then we'll see how far we've got."

That was one of the nice things about having only three people aboard: We didn't have to worry about water discipline very much. It's astonishing how a quick wet-down revives you after coming out of a hotsuit. When I'd finished mine I felt ready for anything.

I was even prepared to eat some of Boyce Cochenour's gourmet cookery, but fortunately it wasn't necessary. The girl had taken over the kitchen, and what she laid out was simple, light, and reasonably non-toxic. On cooking like hers I might be able to survive long enough to collect my charter fee. It crossed my mind for a moment to wonder what made her do it; and then I thought, of course, she'd had a lot of practice. With all the spare parts in Cochenour, no doubt he had dietary problems far worse than mine.

Well, not "worse," exactly, in the sense that I didn't think he was quite as likely to die of them.

According to the autosonic probes, the highest point of the tunnel I had marked "A," or of whatever it was that had seemed like tunnels to their shock waves, was close to the little blind valley in which I'd tied down.

That was very lucky. It meant that we might very possibly be right over the Heechee's own entrance.

The reason that was lucky was not that we would be able to use it the way the Heechee had used it. There wasn't much chance that its mechanisms would have survived a quarter of a million years, much of it exposed to surface wind, ablation, and chemical corrosion. The good part was that if the tunnel had surfaced here it would be relatively easy to bore down to it. Even a quarter of a million years doesn't produce really hard rock, especially without surface water to dissolve out solids and produce compact sediments.

Up to a point, it turned out pretty much the way I had hoped. What was on the surface was little more than ashy sand, and the augers chewed it out very rapidly. Too rapidly; when I went back into the igloo it was filled almost solid with castings, and I had a devil of a job getting to the machines to switch the auger over to pumping the castings out through the crawl lock.

It was a dull, dirty part of the job, but it didn't take long.

I didn't bother to go back into the airbody. I reported what was happening over the radio to Boyce and the girl, staring out the ports at me. I told them I thought we were getting close.

But I didn't tell them exactly how close. Actually, we were only a meter or two from the indicated depth of the anomaly, so close that I didn't bother to pump out all of the castings. I just made enough room to maneuver around, then re-directed the augers; and in five minutes the castings were beginning to come up with the pale blue glimmer that was the sign of a Heechee tunnel.

VIII

About ten minutes after that I keyed on my helmet transmitter and shouted: "Boyce! Dorrie! We've hit a tunnel!"

Either they were sitting around in their suits or they dressed faster than any maze-rat. I unsealed the crawl-through and wiggled out to help them, and they were already coming out of the airbody, staggering against the wind over to me.

They were both yelling questions and congratulations, but I stopped them. "Inside," I ordered. "See for yourself." As a matter of fact, they didn't have to go that far. They could see the color as soon as they knelt to enter the crawl-through.

I followed, and sealed the lock behind me. The reason for that is simple enough. As long as the tunnel isn't breached, it doesn't matter what you do. But the interior of a Heechee tunnel that has remained inviolate is at a pressure only slightly above Earth-normal. Without the sealed dome, the minute you crack the casing you let the whole 20,000-millibar atmosphere of Venus pour in, heat and ablation and all. If the tunnel is empty, or if what's in it is simple, sturdy stuff, there might not be any harm. But if you hit the jackpot you can destroy in half a second what has waited for a quarter of a million years.

We gathered around the shaft and I pointed down. The augers had left a clean shaft, about seventy centimeters by a little over a hundred, with rounded ends. At the bottom you could see the cold blue glow of the outside of the tunnel, only pocked and blotched by the loose castings I hadn't bothered to get out.

"Now what?" demanded Boyce. His voice was hoarse with excitement, which was, I guessed, natural enough.

"Now we burn our way in."

I backed my clients away as far as they could get, pressed against the remaining heap of castings, and unlimbered the fire-jets. I'd already hung sheer-legs over the shaft, and they went right down on their cable with no trouble until they were a few centimeters above the round of the tunnel. Then I fired them up.

You wouldn't think that anything a human being

might do would change the temperature of the surface of Venus, but those fire-drills were something special. In the small space of the igloo the heat flamed up and around us, and our hotsuit cooling systems were overloaded in seconds.

Dorrie gasped, "Oh! I—I think I'm going to—"

Cochenour grabbed her. "Faint if you want to," he said fiercely, "but don't get sick. Walthers! How long does this go on?"

It was as hard for me as it was for them; practice doesn't get you used to something like standing in front of a blast furnace with the doors off the hinges. "Maybe a minute," I gasped. "Hold on—it's all right."

It actually took a little more than that, maybe ninety seconds; my suit telltales were shouting alarm for more than half of the time. But they were built for these overloads, and as long as we didn't cook, the suits wouldn't take any permanent harm.

Then we were through. A half-meter circular section sagged, fell at one side and hung there.

I turned off the firejets, and we all breathed hard for a couple of minutes, while the suit coolers gradually caught up with the load.

"Wow," said Dorotha. "That was pretty rough."

I looked at Cochenour. In the light that splashed up out of the shaft I could see he was frowning. I didn't say anything. I just gave the jets another five-second burn to cut away the rest of the circular section, and it fell free into the tunnel. We could hear it clatter against the floor.

Then I turned on my helmet radio. "There's no pressure differential," I said.

The frown didn't change, nor did he speak.

"Which means this one has been breached," I went on. "Let's go back to the airbody and take a break before we do anything else."

Dorotha shrieked, "Audee! What's the matter with you? I want to go down there and see what's inside!"

Cochenour said bitterly, "Shut up, Dorrie. Don't you hear what he's saying? This one's a dud."

Well, there's always the chance that a breached tunnel opened up to a seismological invasion, not a maze-rat with a cutting torch, and if so, there might be something worthwhile in it anyway. And I didn't have the heart to kill all Dorotha's enthusiasm with one blow.

So we did swing down the cable, one by one, into the Heechee dig, and look around.

It was wholly bare, as most of them are, as far as we could see. That wasn't actually very far, for the other thing wrong with a breached tunnel is that you need pretty good equipment to explore it. With the overloads they'd already had, our suits were all right for a couple hours but not much more than that, and when we tramped about half a mile down the tunnel without finding a thing, they were both willing to tramp back and return to the airbody.

We cleaned up and made ourselves something to drink. Even squandering more of the water reserves on showers didn't do much for our spirits.

We had to eat, but Cochenour didn't bother with his gourmet exhibition. Silently, Dorotha threw tabs into the radar oven, and we fed gloomily on emergency rations.

"Well, that's only the first one," she said at last, determined to be sunny about it. "And it's only our second day."

Cochenour said, "Shut up, Dorrie; the one thing I'm not is a good loser." He was staring at the probe trace. "Walthers, how many tunnels are unmarked but empty, like this one?"

"How can I answer a question like that? If they're unmarked, there's no record of them."

"So those traces don't mean anything. We might dig one a day for the next three weeks and find every one a dud."

I nodded. "We surely might, Boyce."

He looked at me alertly. "And?"

"And that's not the worst part of it. I've taken parties out to dig who would've gone mad with joy to open even a breached tunnel. It's perfectly possible to dig every day for weeks and never hit a real Heechee tunnel at all. Don't knock it; at least you got some action for your money."

"I told you, Walthers, I'm not a loser. Second place is no good." He thought for a minute, then barked: "You picked this spot. Did you know what you were doing?"

Did I? The only way to answer that question would be to find a live one, of course. I could have told him about the months of studying records from the first landings on. I could have mentioned how much trouble I went to, and how many regulations I broke, to get the military survey reports, or how far I'd traveled to talk to the Defense crews who'd been on those early digs. I might have let him know how hard it had been to locate old Jorolemon Hegramet, now teaching exotic archeology back in Tennessee, and how many times we'd corresponded; but all I said was, "The fact that we found one tunnel shows I knew my business as a guide. That's all you paid for. It's up to you if we keep looking or not."

He looked at his thumbnail, considering.

The girl said cheerfully, "Buck up, Boyce. Look at all the other chances we've got—and even if we miss, it'll still be fun telling everybody about it back in Cincinnati."

He didn't even look at her, just said, "Isn't there any way to tell whether a tunnel has been breached or not without going inside?"

"Sure," I said. "You can tell by tapping the outside shell. You can hear the difference in the sound."

"But you have to dig down to it first?"

"Right."

We left it at that, and I got back into my hotsuit to strip away the now useless igloo so that we could move the drills.

I didn't really want to discuss it anymore, because I didn't want him to ask a question that I might want to lie about. I try the best I can to tell the truth, because it's easier to remember what you've said that way.

On the other hand, I'm not fanatic about it, and I don't see that it's any of my business to correct a mistaken impression. For instance, obviously Cochenour and the girl had the impression that I hadn't bothered to sound the tunnel casing because we'd already dug down to it and it was just as easy to cut in.

But, of course, I had tested it. That was the first thing I did as soon as the drill got down that far. And when I heard the high-pressure *thunk* it broke my heart. I had to wait a couple of minutes before I could call them to tell them that we'd reached the outer casing.

At that time, I had not quite faced up to the question of just what I would have done if it had turned out that the tunnel had not been breached.

IX

Cochenour and Dorrie Keefer were maybe the fiftieth or sixtieth party I'd taken on a Heechee dig, and I wasn't surprised that they were willing to work like coolies. I don't care how lazy and bored they start out, by the time they actually come close to finding something that belonged to an almost completely unknown alien race, left there when the closest thing to a human being on Earth was a slope-browed furry little beast killing other beasts with antelope bones, they begin to burn with exploration fever.

So they worked hard, and drove me hard, and I was as eager as they. Maybe more so, as the days went past and I found myself rubbing my right side, just under the short ribs, more and more of the time.

The military boys overflew us half a dozen times in the first few days. They didn't say much, just formal requests for identification, which they already well knew, then away. Regulations say if you find anything you're supposed to report it right away. Over Cochenour's objections, I reported finding that first breached tunnel, which surprised them a little, I think.

And that's all we had to report.

Site B was a pegmatite dike. The other two fairly bright ones, that I called D and E, showed nothing at all when we dug, meaning that the sound reflections had probably been caused by nothing more than invisible interfaces in layers of rock or ash or gravel. I vetoed trying to dig C, the best looking of the bunch. Cochenour gave me a hell of an argument about it, but I held out. The military were still looking in on us every now and then, and I didn't want to get any closer to their perimeter than we already were. I half-promised that, if we didn't have any luck elsewhere in the mascons, we'd sneak back to C for a quick dig before returning to the Spindle, and we left it at that.

We lifted the airbody, moved to a new position, and set out a new pattern of probes.

By the end of the second week we had dug nine times and come up empty every time. We were getting low on igloos and probes. We'd run out of tolerance for each other completely.

Cochenour had turned sullen and savage. I hadn't planned on liking the man much when I first met him, but I hadn't expected him to be as bad as that. Considering that it had to be only a game with him—with all his money, the extra fortune he might pick up by discovering some new Heechee artifacts couldn't have meant anything but extra points on a score pad—he was playing for blood.

I wasn't particularly graceful myself, for that matter. The plain fact was that the pills from the Quackery weren't helping as much as they should. My mouth tasted like rats had nested in it, I was getting headaches, and I was beginning to knock things over. See, the thing about the liver is that it sort of regulates your internal diet. It filters out poisons, it converts some of the carbohydrates into other carbohydrates that you can use, it patches together amino acids into proteins. If it isn't working, you die. The doctor had been all over it with me, and I could visualize what was going on inside me, the mahogany-red cells dying and being replaced by clusters of fat and yellowish matter. It was an ugly kind of picture. The ugliest part was that there wasn't anything I could do about it. Only go on taking pills, and they wouldn't work past a matter of a few days more. Liver, by-by; hepatic failure, hello.

So we were a bad bunch. Cochenour was a bastard because it was his nature to be a bastard, and I was a bastard because I was sick and desperate. The only decent human being aboard was the girl.

She did her best, she really did. She was sometimes sweet and often even pretty, and she was always ready to meet the power people, Cochenour and me, more than halfway. It was clearly tough on her. She was

179

only a kid. No matter how grownup she acted, she just hadn't been alive long enough to grow a defense against concentrated meanness. Add in the fact that we were all beginning to hate the sight and sound and smell of each other (and in an airbody you get to know a lot about how people smell). There wasn't much joy on Venus for Dorrie Keefer.

Or for any of us, especially after I broke the news that we were down to our last igloo.

Cochenour cleared his throat. He sounded like a fighter-plane jockey blowing the covers off his guns in preparation for combat, and Dorrie attempted to head him off with a diversion. "Audee," she said brightly, "you know what I think we could do? We could go back to that site that looked good near the military reservation."

It was the wrong diversion. I shook my head. "No."

"What the hell do you mean, 'No'?" rumbled Cochenour, revving up for battle.

"What I said. No. That's a desperation trick, and I'm not that desperate."

"Walthers," he snarled, "you'll be desperate when I tell you to be desperate. I can still stop payment on that check."

"No, you can't. The union won't let you. The regulations are very clear about that. You pay up unless I disobey a lawful directive; you can't make me do anything against the law, and going inside the military reservation is extremely against the law."

He shifted over to cold war. "No," he said softly, "you're wrong about that. It's only against the law if a court says it is, after we do it. You're only right if your lawyers are smarter than my lawyers. Honestly, Walthers, I pay my lawyers to be the smartest there are."

The difficult part was that he was even more right than he knew he was, because my liver was on his side. I couldn't spare time for arbitration because without his money and my transplant I wouldn't live that long.

Dorrie, listening with her birdlike look of friendly interest, got between us again. "Well, then, how about this? We just put down here. Why don't we wait and see what the probes show? Maybe we'll hit something even better than that Trace C—"

"There isn't going to be anything good here," he said without looking at her.

"Why, Boyce, how do you know that? We haven't even finished the soundings."

He said, "Look, Dorotha, listen close one time and then shut up. Walthers is playing games. You see where we are now?"

He brushed past me and tapped out the program for a full map display, which somewhat surprised me because I didn't know he knew how. The charts sprang up with virtual images of our position, the shafts we'd already cut, the great irregular edge of the military reservation overlaid on the plot of mascons and navigation aids.

"You see? We're not even in the high-density mass areas now. Is that true, Walthers? We've tried all the good locations and come up dry?"

I said, "You're partly right, Mr. Cochenour, but I'm not playing games. This site is a good possibility. You can see it on the map. We're not over any mascon, that's true, but we're right between two of them that are located pretty close together. Sometimes you find a dig that connects two complexes, and it has happened that the connecting passage was closer to the surface than any other part of the system. I can't guarantee we'll hit anything here, but it's not impossible."

181

"Just damn unlikely?"

"Well, no more unlikely than anywhere else. I told you a week ago, you got your money's worth the first day just finding any Heechee tunnel at all, even a spoiled one. There are maze-rats in the Spindle who went five years without seeing that much." I thought for a minute. "I'll make a deal with you," I said.

"I'm listening."

"We're down here, and there's at least a chance we can hit something. Let's try. We'll deploy the probes and see what they turn up. If we get a good trace we'll dig it. If we don't—then I'll think about going back to Trace C."

"Think about it!" he roared.

"Don't push me, Cochenour. You don't know what you're getting into. The military reservation is not to be fooled with. Those boys shoot first and ask later, and there aren't any policemen or courts on Venus to even ask them questions."

"I don't know," he said after a moment.

"No," I said, "you don't, Mr. Cochenour, and that's what you're paying me for. I do know."

"Yes," he agreed, "you probably do, but whether you're telling me the truth about what you know is another question. Hegramet never said anything about digging between mascons."

And then he looked at me with a completely opaque expression, waiting to see whether I would catch him up on what he had just said.

I didn't respond. I gave him an opaque look back. I didn't say a word; I only waited to see what would come next. I was pretty sure that it would not be any sort of explanation of how he happened to know Hegramet's name, or what dealings he had had with the greatest Earthside authority on Heechee diggings, and it wasn't.

"Put out your probes and we'll try it your way one more time," he said at last.

I plopped the probes out, got good penetration on all of them, started firing the noisemakers. I sat watching the first buildup of lines on the scan as though I expected them to carry useful information. They couldn't, of course, but it was a good excuse to think privately for a moment.

Cochenour needed to be thought about. He hadn't come to Venus just for the ride, that was clear. He had known he was going to be sinking shafts after Heechee digs before he ever left Earth. He had briefed himself on the whole bit, even to handling the instruments on the airbody. My sales talk about Heechee treasures had been wasted on a customer whose mind had been made up to buy at least half a year earlier and tens of millions of miles away.

All that I understood, but the more I understood the more I saw that I didn't understand. What I really wanted was to give Cochenour a quarter and send him to the movies for a while so I could talk privately to the girl. Unfortunately, there was nowhere to send him. I managed to force a yawn, complain about the boredom of waiting for the probe traces to build up, and suggest a nap. Not that I would have been real confident he wasn't lying there with his ears flapping, listening to us. It didn't matter. Nobody acted sleepy but me. All I got out of it was an offer from Dorrie to watch the screen and wake me if anything interesting turned up.

So I said the hell with it and went to sleep myself.

It was not a good sleep, because lying there waiting for it gave me time to notice how truly lousy I felt, and in how many ways. There was a sort of permanent taste of bile in the back of my mouth, not so much as though I wanted to throw up as it was as though I just had. My head ached, and I was beginning to see ghost images wandering fuzzily around my field of vision. When I took my pills I didn't count the ones that were left. I didn't want to know.

I'd set my private alarm for three hours, thinking maybe that would give Cochenour time to get sleepy and turn in, leaving the girl up and about and perhaps conversational. But when I woke up there was Cochenour, cooking himself an herb omelette with the last of our sterile eggs. "You were right, Walthers," he grinned, "I was sleepy. Had a nice little nap. Ready for anything now. Want some eggs?"

Actually I did want them; but of course I didn't dare eat them, so I glumly swallowed what the Quackery had allowed me to have and watched him stuff himself. It was unfair that a man of ninety could be so healthy that he didn't have to think about digestion, while I was—well, there wasn't any profit in that kind of thinking, so I offered to play some music, and Dorrie picked *Swan Lake,* and I started it up.

And then I had an idea and headed for the tool lockers. They needed checking. The auger heads were about due for replacement, and I knew we were low on spares; and the other thing about the tool lockers was that they were as far from the galley as you could get and stay inside the airbody, and I hoped Dorrie would follow me. And she did.

"Need any help, Audee?"

"Glad to have it," I said. "Here, hold these for me. Don't get the grease on your clothes." I didn't expect her to ask me why they had to be held. She didn't. She only laughed.

"Grease? I don't think I'd even notice it, dirty as I am. I guess we're all about ready to get back to civilization."

Cochenour was frowning over the probe trace and paying us no attention. I said, "Meaning which kind of civilization, the Spindle or Earth."

What I had in mind was to start her talking about Earth, but she went the other way. "Oh, the Spindle, Audee. I thought it was fascinating, and we really didn't get to see much of it. And the people. Like that Indian fellow who ran the cafe. The cashier was his wife, wasn't she?"

"One of them. She's the number-one wife; the waitress was number three, and he has another one at home with the kids. There are five of them, all three wives involved." But I wanted to go in the other direction, so I said, "It's pretty much the same as on Earth. Vastra would be running a tourist trap in Benares if he wasn't running one here, and he wouldn't be here if he hadn't shipped out with the military and terminated here. I'd be guiding in Texas, I suppose. If there's any open country left to guide in, maybe up along the Canadian River. How about you?"

All the time I was picking up the same four or five tools, studying the serial numbers and putting them back. She didn't notice.

"How do you mean?"

"Well, what did you do before you came here?"

"Oh, I worked in Boyce's office for a while."

That was encouraging; maybe she'd remember something about his connection with Professor Hegramet. "What were you, a secretary?"

"Something like that. Boyce let me handle—oh, what's that?"

That was an incoming call on the radio, that was what that was.

"So go answer," snarled Cochenour from across the airbody.

I took it on the earjack, since that is my nature; there

isn't any privacy to speak of in an airbody, and I want what little crumbs of it I can find. It was the base calling, a comm sergeant I knew named Littleknees. I signed in irritably, regretting the chance to pump Dorotha about her boss.

"A private word for you, Audee," said Sergeant Littleknees. "Got your sahib around?"

Littleknees and I had exchanged radio chatter for a long time, and there was something about the cheerfulness of the tone that bothered me. I didn't look at Cochenour, but I knew he was listening—only to my side, of course, because of the earjack. "In sight but not receiving," I said. "What have you got for me?"

"Just a little news bulletin," the sergeant purred. "It came over the synsat net a couple of minutes ago. Information only. That means we don't have to do anything about it, but maybe you do, honey."

"Standing by," I said, studying the plastic housing of the radio.

The sergeant chuckled. "Your sahib's charter captain would like to have a word with him when found. It's kind of urgent, 'cause the captain is righteously kissed off."

"Yes, base," I said. "Your signals received, strength ten."

The sergeant made an amused noise again, but this time it wasn't a chuckle, it was a downright giggle. "The thing is," she said, "his check for the charter fee bounced. Want to know what the bank said? You'd never guess. 'Insufficient funds,' that's what they said."

The pain under my right lower ribs was permanent, but right then it seemed to get a lot worse. I gritted my teeth. "Ah, Sergeant Littleknees," I croaked, "can you, ah, verify that estimate?"

"Sorry, honey," she buzzed sympathetically in my ear, "but there's no doubt in the world. Captain got a credit report on him and it turned up n.g. When your customer gets back to the Spindle there'll be a make-good warrant waiting for him."

"Thank you for the synoptic report," I said hollowly. "I will verify departure time before we take off."

And I turned off the radio and gazed at my rich billionaire client.

"What the hell's the matter with you, Walthers?" he growled.

But I wasn't hearing his voice. I was hearing what the happy fellow at the Quackery had told me. The equations were unforgettable. Cash $=$ new liver $+$ happy survival. No cash $=$ total hepatic failure $+$ death. And my cash supply had just dried up.

X

When you get a really big piece of news you have to let it trickle through your system and get thoroughly absorbed before you do anything about it. It isn't a matter of seeing the implications. I saw them right away, you bet. It's a matter of letting the system reach an equilibrium state. So I puttered for a minute. I listened to Tschaikovsky. I made sure the radio switch was off so as not to waste power. I checked the synoptic plot. It would have been nice if there had been something to show, but, the way things were going, there wouldn't be, of course, and there wasn't. A few pale echoes were building up. But nothing with the shape of a Heechee dig, and nothing very bright. The data were still coming in, but there was no way for those feeble plots to turn into the mother-lode that could save us all, even broke bastard Cochenour. I even looked out at as much of the sky as I could to see how the weather was. It didn't matter, but some of the high white calomel clouds were scudding among the purples and yellows of the other mercury halides. It was beautiful and I hated it.

Cochenour had forgotten about his omelette and was watching me thoughtfully. So was Dorrie, still holding the augers in their grease-paper wrap. I grinned at her. "Pretty," I said, referring to the music. The Auckland Philharmonic was just getting to the part where the little swans come out arm in arm and do a fast, bouncy *pas de quatre* across the stage. It has always been one of my favorite parts of *Swan Lake*. "We'll listen to the rest of it later," I said, and snapped it off.

"All right," snarled Cochenour, "what's going on?"

I sat down on an igloo pack and lit a cigarette, because one of the adjustments my internal system had made was to calculate that we didn't have to worry much about coddling our oxygen supply any more. I said. "There's a question that's bothering me, Cochenour. How did you get on to Professor Hegramet?"

He grinned and relaxed. "Is that all that's on your mind? I checked the place out before I came. Why not?"

"No reason, except that you let me think you didn't know a thing."

He shrugged. "If you had any brains you'd know I didn't get rich by being stupid. You think I'd come umpty-million miles without knowing what I was coming to?"

"No, you wouldn't, but you did your best to make me think you would. No matter. So you dug up somebody who could point you to whatever was worth stealing on Venus, and somebody steered you to Hegramet. Then what? Did he tell you I was dumb enough to be your boy?"

Cochenour wasn't quite as relaxed, but he wasn't aggressive either. He said, "Hegramet told me you were the right guide to find a virgin tunnel. That's all —except briefing on the Heechee and so on. If you hadn't come to us I would have come to you; you just saved me the trouble."

I said, a little surprised, "You know, I think you're telling me the truth. Except you left out one thing: It wasn't the fun of making more money that you were after, it was just money, right? Money that you needed." I turned to Dorotha, standing frozen with the augers in her hand. "How about it, Dorrie? Did you know the old man was broke?"

Putting it that way was not too smart. I saw what she was about to do just before she did it, and jumped off the igloo. I was a little too late. She dropped the augers before I could get them from her, but fortunately they landed flat and the blades weren't chipped. I picked them up and put them away.

She had answered the question well enough.

I said, "I see you didn't know. Tough on you, doll. His check to the captain of the *Gagarin* is still bouncing, and I would imagine the one he gave me isn't going to be much better. I hope you got it in furs and jewels, and my advice to you is to hide them before the creditors want them back."

She didn't even look at me. She was only looking at Cochenour, whose expression was all the confirmation she needed.

I don't know what I expected from her, rage or reproaches or tears. What she did was whisper, "Oh, Boyce, I'm so sorry," and she went over and put her arm around him.

I turned my back on them, because I didn't like looking at him. The strapping ninety-year-old buck on Full Medical had turned into a defeated old man. For the first time, he looked all of his age and maybe a little more: the mouth half open, trembling; the straight back stooped; the bright blue eyes watering. She stroked him and crooned to him.

I looked at the synoptic web again, for lack of anything better to do. It was about as clear as it was going to get, and it was empty. We had nearly a fifty percent overlap from our previous soundings, so I could tell that the interesting-looking scratches at one edge were nothing to get excited about. We'd checked them out already. They were only ghosts.

There was no rescue there.

Curiously, I felt kind of relaxed. There is something tranquilizing about the realization that you have nothing much left to lose. It puts things in a different perspective. I don't mean to say that I had given up completely. There were still things I could do. They might not have anything to do with prolonging my life, but the taste in my mouth and the pain in my gut weren't letting me enjoy life very much anyway. I could, for instance, write Audee Walthers off; since only a miracle could keep me from dying in a matter of days, I could accept the fact that I wasn't going to be alive a week from now and use what time I had for something else. What else? Well, Dorrie was a nice kid. I could fly the airbody back to the Spindle, turn Cochenour over to the gendarmes, and spend my last day or so introducing her around. Vastra or BeeGee would help her get organized. She might not even have to go into prostitution or the rackets. The high season wasn't that far off, and she would do well with a little booth of prayer fans and Heechee lucky pieces for the Terry tourists. Maybe that wasn't much, even from her point of view, but it was something.

Or I could fling myself on the mercy of the Quackery. They might let me have the new liver on credit. The only reason I had for thinking they wouldn't was that they never had.

Or I could open the two-fuel valves and let them mix for ten minutes or so before hitting the igniter. The explosion wouldn't leave much of the airbody or us, and nothing at all of our problems.

Or—

"Oh, hell," I said. "Buck up, Cochenour. We're not dead yet."

He looked at me for a minute. He patted Dorrie's shoulder and pushed her away, gently enough. He said, "I will be, soon enough. I'm sorry about all this, Dorotha. And I'm sorry about your check, Walthers; I expect you needed the money."

"You have no idea."

He said with difficulty, "Do you want me to explain?"

"I don't see that it makes any difference, but, yes, out of curiosity I do."

I let him tell me, and he did it steadily and succinctly. I could have guessed. A man his age is either very, very rich or dead. He was only quite rich. He'd kept his industries going on what was left after he siphoned off the costs of transplant and treatment, calciphylaxis and prosthesis, protein regeneration here, cholesterol flushing there, a million for this, a hundred grand a week for that . . . oh, it went, I could see that. "You just don't know," he said, "what it takes to keep a hundred-year-old man alive until you try it."

I corrected him automatically. "Ninety, you mean."

"No, not ninety, and not even a hundred. I think it's at least a hundred and ten, and it could be more than that. Who counts? You pay the doctors and they patch you up for a month or two. You wouldn't know."

Oh, wouldn't I just, I said, but not out loud. I let him go on, telling about how the federal inspectors were closing in and he skipped Earth to make his fortune all over again on Venus.

But I wasn't listening any more; I was writing on the back of a navigation form. When I was finished, I passed it over to Cochenour. "Sign it," I said.

"What is it?"

"Does it matter? You don't have any choice, do you? But it's a release from the all-rights section of our charter agreement; you acknowledge you have no claim, that your check's rubber, and that you voluntarily waive your ownership of anything we find in my favor."

He frowned. "What's this bit at the end?"

"That's where I give you ten percent of anything we do find, *if* we do find anything."

"That's charity," he said, but he was signing. "I don't mind charity, especially since, as you point out, I don't have any choice. But I can read that web as well as you can, Walthers, and there's nothing on it to find."

"No," I said, folding the paper and putting it in my pocket, "But we're not going to dig here. That trace is bare as your bank account. What we're going to do is dig Trace C."

I lit another cigarette and thought for a minute. I was wondering how much to tell them of what I had spent five years finding out and figuring out, schooling myself not even to hint at it to anyone else. I was sure in my mind that nothing I said would make a difference, but the words didn't want to say themselves anyway.

I made myself say:

"You remember Subhash Vastra, the fellow who ran the trap where I met you. He came to Venus with the military. He was a weapons specialist. There's no civilian career for a weapons specialist so he went into the cafe business when they terminated him, but he was pretty big at it in the service."

Dorrie said, "Do you mean there are Heechee weapons on the reservation?"

"No. Nobody has ever found a Heechee weapon. But they found targets."

It was actually physically difficult for me to speak the next part, but I got it out. "Anyway, Sub Vastra says they were targets. The higher brass wasn't sure, and I think the matter has been pigeonholed on the reservation by now. But what they found was triangular pieces of Heechee wall material—that blue, light-emitting stuff they lined the tunnels with. There were dozens of them, and they all had a pattern of radiating lines; Sub said they looked like targets to him. And they had been drilled through, by something that left the holes chalky as talc. Do you know anything that would do that to Heechee wall material?"

Dorrie was about to say she didn't, but Cochenour interrupted her. "That's impossible," he said flatly.

"Right, that's what the brass said. They decided it had to be done in the process of fabrication, for some Heechee purpose we'll never know. But Vastra says not. He says they looked exactly like the paper targets from the firing range under the reservation. The holes weren't all in the same place; the lines looked like scoring markers. That's evidence he's right. Not proof. But evidence."

"And you think you can find the gun that made those holes where we marked Trace C?"

I hesitated. "I wouldn't put it that strongly. Call it a hope. But there is one more thing.

"These targets were turned up by a prospector nearly forty years ago. He turned them in, reported his find, went out looking for more and got killed. That happened a lot in those days. No one paid much attention until some military types got a look at them; and that's how come the reservation is where it is. They spotted the site where he'd reported finding them, staked out everything for a thousand kilometers around and labeled it all off limits. And they dug and dug, turned up about a dozen Heechee tunnels, but most of them bare and the rest cracked and spoiled."

"Then there's nothing there," growled Cochenour, looking perplexed.

"There's nothing they found," I corrected him. "But in those days prospectors lied a lot. He reported the wrong location for the find. At the time, he was shacked up with a young lady who later married a man named Allemang, and her son is a friend of mine. He had a map. The right location, as near as I can figure—the navigation marks weren't what they are now—is right about where we are now, give or take some. I saw digging marks a couple of times and I think they were his." I slipped the little private magnetofiche out of my pocket and put it into the virtual map display; it showed a single mark, an orange X. "That's where I think we might find the weapon, somewhere near that X. And as you can see, the only undug indication there is good old Trace C."

Silence for a minute. I listened to the distant outside howl of the winds, waiting for them to say something.

Dorrie was looking troubled. "I don't know if I like trying to find a new weapon," she said. "It's—it's like bringing back the bad old days again."

I shrugged. Cochenour, beginning to look more like himself again, said, "The point isn't whether we really want to find a weapon, is it? The point is that we want to find an untapped Heechee dig for whatever is in it —but the soldiers think there *might* be a weapon some-where around, so they aren't going to let us dig, right?

They'll shoot us first and ask questions later. Wasn't that what you said?"

"That's what I said."

"So how do you propose to get around that little problem?" he asked.

If I were a truthful man I would have said I wasn't sure I could. Looked at honestly, the odds were we would get caught and very likely shot; but we had so little to lose, Cochenour and I, that I didn't think that important enough to mention. I said:

"We try to fool them. We send the airbody off, and you and I stay behind to do the digging. If they think we're gone, they won't be keeping us under surveillance, and all we have to worry about is being picked up on a routine perimeter search."

"Audee!" cried the girl. "If you and Boyce stay here— But that means I have to take the airbody, and *I* can't fly this thing."

"No, you can't. But you can let it fly itself." I rushed on: "Oh, you'll waste fuel and you'll get bounced around a lot. But you'll get there on autopilot. It'll even land you at the Spindle." Not necessarily easily or well; I closed my mind to the thought of what an automatic landing might do to my one and only airbody. She would survive it, though, ninety-nine chances out of a hundred.

"Then what?" Cochenour demanded.

There were big holes in the plan at this point, but I closed my mind to them, too. "Dorrie looks up my friend BeeGee Allemang. I'll give you a note to give him with all the coordinates and so on, and he'll come and pick us up. With extra tanks, we'll have air and power for maybe forty-eight hours after you leave. That's plenty of time for you to get there, find BeeGee and give him the message, and for him to get back. If he's late, of course, we're in trouble. If we don't find anything, we've wasted our time. But if we do—"

I shrugged. "I didn't say it was a guarantee," I added, "I only said it gave us a chance."

Dorrie was quite a nice person, considering her age and her circumstances, but one of the things she lacked was self-confidence. She had not been trained to it; she had been getting it as a prosthesis, from Cochenour most recently, I suppose before that from whoever preceded Cochenour in her life—at her age, maybe her father.

That was the biggest problem, persuading Dorrie she could do her part. "It won't work," she kept saying. "I'm sorry. It isn't that I don't want to help. I do, but I can't. It just won't work."

Well, it would have.

Or at least I think it would have.

In the event, we never got to try it. Between us, Cochenour and I did get Dorrie to agree to give it a try. We packed up what little gear we'd put outside, flew back to the ravine, landed and began to set up for the dig. But I was feeling poorly, thick, headachy, clumsy, and I suppose Cochenour had his own problems. Between the two of us we managed to catch the casing of the drill in the exit port while we were off-loading it, and while I was jockeying it one way from above, Cochenour pulled the other way from beneath and the whole thing came down on top of him. It didn't kill him. But it gouged his suit and broke his leg, and that took care of my idea of digging Trace C with him.

XI

The suit leg had been ruptured through eight or ten plies, but there was enough left to keep the air out, if not the pressure.

The first thing I did was check the drill to make sure it wasn't damaged. It wasn't. The second thing was to fight Cochenour back into the lock. That took about everything I had, with the combined weight of our suits and bodies, getting the drill out of the way, and my general physical condition. But I managed it.

Dorrie was great. No hysterics, no foolish questions. We got him out of his suit and looked him over. He was unconscious. The leg was compounded, with bone showing through; he was bleeding from the mouth and nose, and he had vomited inside his helmet. All in all he was about the worst-looking hundred-and-some-year-old man you'll ever see—live one, anyway. But he hadn't taken enough heat to cook his brain, his heart was still going—well, whoever's heart it had been in the first place, I mean; it was a good investment, because it pumped right along. The bleeding stopped by itself, except from the nasty business on the leg.

Dorrie called the military reservation for me, got Eve Littleknees, was put right through to the Base Surgeon. He told me what to do. At first he wanted me to pack up and bring Cochenour right over, but I vetoed that— said I wasn't in shape to fly and it would be too rough a ride. Then he gave me step-by-steps and I followed it easily enough: reduced the fracture, packed the gash, closed the wound with surgical Velcro and meat glue, sprayed a bandage all around and poured on a cast. It took about an hour, and Cochenour would have come to while we were doing it except I gave him a sleepy needle.

So then it was just a matter of taking pulse and respiration and blood-pressure readings to satisfy the surgeon, and promising to get him back to the Spindle shortly. When the surgeon was through, still annoyed at me for not bringing Cochenour over, Sergeant Littleknees came back on. I could tell what was on her mind.

"Uh, honey? How did it happen?"

"A great big Heechee came up out of the ground and bit him," I said. "I know what you're thinking and you've got an evil mind. It was just an accident."

"Sure," she said. "Okay. I just wanted you to know I don't blame you a bit." And she signed off.

Dorrie was cleaning Cochenour up as best she could —pretty profligate with the water reserves, I thought. I left her to it while I made myself some coffee, lit a cigarette, and sat and thought.

By the time Dorrie had done what she could for Cochenour, then cleaned up the worst of the mess and begun to do such important tasks as repairing her eye makeup, I had thought up a dandy.

I gave Cochenour a wake-up needle, and Dorrie patted him and talked to him while he got his bearings. She was not a girl who carried a grudge. I did, a little. I got him up to try out his muscles faster than he really wanted to. His expression told me that they all ached. They worked all right, though.

He was able to grin. "Old bones," he said. "I knew I should have gone for the recalciphylaxis. That's what happens when you try to save a buck."

He sat down heavily, the leg stuck out in front of him. He wrinkled his nose. "Sorry to have messed up your nice clean airbody," he aded.

"You want to clean yourself up?"

He looked surprised. "Well, I think I'd better, pretty soon—"

"Do it now. I want to talk to you both."

He didn't argue, just held out his hand, and Dorrie took it. He stumped, half-hopped toward the clean-up. Actually Dorrie had done the worst of it, but he splashed a little water on his face and swished some around in his mouth. He was pretty well recovered when he turned around to look at me.

"All right, what is it? Are we giving up?"

I said. "No. We'll do it a different way."

Dorrie cried, "He can't, Audee! Look at him. And the condition his suit's in, he couldn't last outside an hour, much less help you dig."

"I know that, so we'll have to change the plan. I'll dig by myself. The two of you will slope off in the airbody."

"Oh, brave man," said Cochenour flatly. "Who are you kidding? It's a two-man job."

I hesitated. "Not necessarily. Lone prospectors have done it before, although the problems were a little different. I admit it'll be a tough 48 for me, but we'll have to try it. One reason. We don't have any alternative."

"Wrong," said Cochenour. He patted Dorrie's rump. "Solid muscle, that girl. She isn't big, but she's healthy. Takes after her grandmother. Dont argue, Walthers. Just think a little bit. It's as safe for Dorrie as it is for you; and with the two of you, there's a chance we might luck in. By yourself, no chance at all."

For some reason, his attitude put me in a bad temper. "You talk as though she didn't have anything to say about it."

"Well," said Dorrie, sweetly enough, "come to that, so do you. I appreciate your wanting to make things easy for me, Audee, but, honestly, I think I could help. I've learned a lot. And if you want the truth, you look a lot worse than I do."

I said with all the sneer I could get into my voice, "Forget it. You can both help me for an hour or so, while I get set up. Then we'll do it my way. No arguments. Let's get going."

That made two mistakes. The first was that we didn't get set up in an hour; it took more than two, and I was sweating sick oily sweat before we finished. I really felt bad. I was past hurting or worrying about it; I just thought it a little surprising every time my heart beat. Dorrie did more muscle work than I did, strong and willing as promised, and Cochenour checked over the instruments, and asked a couple of questions when he had to to make sure he could handle his part of the job, flying the airbody. I took two cups of coffee heavily laced with my private supply of gin and smoked my last cigarette for a while, meanwhile checking out with the military reservation. Eve Littleknees was flirtatious but a little puzzled.

Then Dorrie and I tumbled out of the lock and closed it behind us, leaving Cochenour strapped in the pilot's seat.

Dorrie stood there for a moment, looking forlorn; but then she grabbed my hand and the two of us lumbered to the shelter of the igloo we'd already ignited. I had impressed on her the importance of being out of the wash of the twin-fuel jets. She was good about it; flung herself flat and didn't move.

I was less cautious. As soon as I could judge from the flare that the jets were angled away from us, I stuck my head up and watched Cochenour take off in a sleet of heavy-metal ash. It wasn't a bad takeoff. In circumstances like that I define "bad" as total demolition of the airbody and the death or maiming of one or more persons. He avoided that, but the airbody skittered and slid wildly as the gusts caught it. It would be a rough ride for him, going just the few hundred kilometers north that would take him out of detection range.

I touched Dorrie with my toe and she struggled up. I slipped the talk cord into the jack on her helmet—

radio was out, because of possible perimeter patrols that we wouldn't be able to see.

"Change your mind yet?" I asked.

It was a fairly obnoxious question, but she took it nicely. She giggled. I could tell that because we were faceplate to faceplate and I could see her face shadowed inside the helmet. But I couldn't hear what she was saying until she remembered to nudge the voice switch, and then what I heard was:

"—romantic, just the two of us."

Well, we didn't have time for that kind of chitchat. I said irritably, "Let's quit wasting time. Remember what I told you. We have air, water and power for 48 hours. Don't count on any margin. One or two of them might hold out a little longer, but you need all three to stay alive. Try not to work too hard; the less you metabolize, the less your waste system has to handle. If we find a tunnel and get in, maybe we can eat some of those emergency rations over there—provided it's unbreached and hasn't heated up too much in a quarter of a million years. Otherwise don't even think about food. As for sleeping, forget—"

"Now who's wasting time? You told me all this before." But she was still cheery.

So we climbed into the igloo and started work.

The first thing we had to do was clear out some of the tailings that had already begun to accumulate where we left the drill going. The usual way, of course, is to reverse and redirect the augers. We couldn't do that. It would have meant taking them away from cutting the shaft. We had to do it the hard way, namely manually.

It was hard, all right. Hotsuits are uncomfortable to begin with. When you have to work in them, they're miserable. When the work is both very hard physically and complicated by the cramped space inside an igloo that already contains two people and a working drill, it's next to impossible.

We did it anyhow, having no choice.

Cochenour hadn't lied; Dorrie was as good as a man. The question was whether that was going to be good enough. The other question, which was bothering me more and more every minute, was whether I was as good as a man. The headache was really pounding at me, and I found myself blacking out when I moved suddenly. The Quackery had promised me three weeks before acute hepatic failure, but that hadn't been meant to include this kind of work. I had to figure I was on plus time already. That is a disconcerting way to figure.

Especially when ten hours went by and I realized that we were down lower than the soundings had shown the tunnel to be, and no luminous blue tailings were in sight.

We were drilling a dry hole.

Now, if we had had the airbody close by, this would have been an annoyance. Maybe a big annoyance, but not a disaster. What I would have done was get back in the airbody, clean up, get a good night's sleep, eat a meal, and recheck the trace. We were digging in the wrong place. All right, next step is to dig in the right place. Study the terrain, pick a spot, ignite another igloo, start up the drills and try, try again.

That's what we *would* have done. But we didn't have any of those advantages. We didn't have the airbody. We had no chance for sleep or food. We were out of igloos. We didn't have the trace to look at. And I was feeling lousier every minute.

I crawled out of the igloo, sat down in the next thing there was to the lee of the wind, and stared at the scudding yellow-green sky.

There ought to be something to do, if I could only think of it. I ordered myself to think.

Well, let's see. Could I maybe uproot the igloo and move it to another spot?

No. I could break it loose all right with the augers, but the minute it was free the winds would catch it and it would be good-by, Charlie. I'd never see that igloo again. Plus there would be no way to make it gastight anyway.

Well, then, how about drilling without an igloo?

Possible, I judged. Pointless, though. Suppose we did hit lucky and hole in? Without an igloo to lock out those twenty thousand millibars of hot gas, we'd destroy the contents anyway.

I felt a nudge on my shoulder, and discovered that Dorrie was sitting next to me. She didn't ask any questions, didn't try to say anything at all. I guess it was all clear enough without talking about it.

By my suit chronometer fifteen hours were gone. That left thirty-some before Cochenour would come back and get us. I didn't see any point in spending it all sitting there, but on the other hand I didn't see any point in doing anything else.

Of course, I thought, I could always go to sleep for a while . . . and then I woke up and realized that that was what I had been doing.

Dorrie was asleep beside me.

You may wonder how a person can sleep in the teeth of a south polar thermal gale. It isn't all that hard. All it takes is that you be wholly worn out, and wholly despairing. Sleeping isn't just to knit the raveled sleeve, it is a good way to shut the world off when the world is too lousy to face. As ours was.

But Venus is the last refuge of the Puritan ethic. Crazy. I knew I was as good as dead, but I felt I had to be doing something. I eased away from Dorrie, made sure her suit was belted to the hold-tight ring at the base of the igloo, and stood up. It took a great deal of concentration for me to be able to stand up, which was almost as good at keeping care out as sleep.

It occurred to me that there still might be eight or ten live Heechees in the tunnel, and maybe they'd heard us knocking and opened up the bottom of the shaft for us. So I crawled into the igloo to see.

I peered down the shaft to make sure. No. They hadn't. It was still just a blind hole that disappeared into dirty dark invisibility at the end of the light from my head lamp. I swore at the Heechees who hadn't helped us out, and kicked some tailings down the shaft on their non-existent heads.

The Puritan ethic was itching me, and I wondered what I ought to do. Die? Well, yes, but I was doing that fast enough. Something constructive?

I remembered that you always ought to leave a place the way you found it, so I hauled up the drills on the eight-to-one winch and stowed them neatly. I kicked some more tailings down the useless hole to make a place to sit, and I sat down and thought.

I mused about what we had done wrong, as you might think about a chess puzzle.

I could still see the trace in my mind. It was bright and clear, so there was definitely something there. It was just tough that we'd lucked out and missed it.

How had we missed it?

After some time, I thought I knew the answer to that.

People like Dorrie and Cochenour have an idea that a seismic trace is like one of those underground maps of downtown Dallas, with all the sewers and utility conduits and water pipes marked, so you just dig where it says and you find what you want.

It isn't exactly like that. The trace comes out as a

sort of hazy approximation. It is built up, hour by hour, by measuring the echoes from the pinger. It looks like a band of spiderweb shadows, much wider than an actual tunnel and very fuzzy at the edges. When you look at it you know that somewhere in the shadows there's something that makes them. Maybe it's a rock interface or a pocket of gravel. Hopefully it's a Heechee dig. Whatever it is, it's there somewhere, but you don't just know where, exactly. If a tunnel is twenty meters wide, which is a fair average for a Heechee connecting link, the shadow trace is sure to look like fifty, and may be a hundred.

So where do you dig?

That's where the art of prospecting comes in. You have to make an informed guess.

Maybe you dig in the exact geometrical center—as far as it is given you to see where the center is. That's the easiest way. Maybe you dig where the shadows are densest, which is the way the half-smart prospectors do, and that works almost half the time. Or maybe you do what I did, and try to think like a Heechee. You look at the trace as a whole and try to see what points they might have been trying to connect. Then you plot an imaginary course between them, where you would have put the tunnel if you had been the Heechee engineer in charge, and you dig somewhere along there.

That's what I had done, but evidently I had done wrong.

In a fuzzy-brained sort of way, I began to think I saw what I'd done.

I visualized the trace. The right place to dig was where I had set the airbody down, but of course I couldn't set up the igloo there because the airbody was in the way. So I'd set up about ten yards upslope.

I was convinced that ten yards was what made us miss.

205

I was pleased with myself for figuring it out, although I couldn't see that it made a lot of practical difference. If I'd had another igloo I would have been glad to try again, assuming I could hold out that long. But that didn't mean much, because I didn't have another igloo.

So I sat on the edge of the dark shaft, nodding sagaciously over the way I had solved the problem, dangling my legs and now and then sweeping tailings in. I think that was part of a kind of death wish, because I know I thought, now and then, that the nicest thing to do would be to jump in and pull the tailings down over me.

But the Puritan ethic didn't want me to do that. Anyway, it would have solved only my own personal problem. It wouldn't have done anything for old Dorrie Keefer, snoring away outside in the thermal hurricane.

I then began to wonder why I was worrying about Dorrie. It was a pleasant enough subject to be thinking about, but sort of sad.

I went back to thinking about the tunnel.

The bottom of the shaft couldn't be more than a few yards away from where we had bottomed out empty. I thought of jumping down and scraping away with my bare gloves. It seemed like a good idea. I'm not sure how much was whimsy and how much the fantasy of a sick man, but I kept thinking how nice it would be if there were Heechees still in there, and when I scratched into the blue wall material I could just knock politely and they'd open up and let me in. I even had a picture of what they looked like: sort of friendly and godlike. It would have been very pleasant to meet a Heechee, a live one that could speak English. "Heechee, what did you really use those things we call prayer fans for?" I could ask him. Or, "Heechee, have you got anything that will keep me from dying in your medicine chest?"

Or, "Heechee, I'm sorry we messed up your front yard and I'll try to clean it up for you."

I pushed more of the tailings back into the shaft. I had nothing better to do, and who could tell, maybe they'd appreciate it. After a while I had it half full and I'd run out of tailings, except for the ones that were pushed outside the igloo, and I didn't have the strength to go after them. I looked for something else to do. I reset the augers, replaced the dull blades with the last sharp ones we had, pointed them in the general direction of a twenty-degree offset angle downslope, and turned them on.

It wasn't until I noticed that Dorrie was standing next to me, helping me steady the augers for the first yards of cut, that I realized I had made a plan.

Why not try an offset cut? Did we have any better chance?

We did not. We cut.

When the drills stopped bucking and settled down to chew into the rock and we could leave them, I cleared a space at the side of the igloo and shoved tailings out for a while; then we just sat there and watched the drills spit rock chips into the old shaft. It was filling up nicely. We didn't speak. Presently I fell asleep again.

I didn't wake up until Dorrie pounded on my head. We were buried in tailings, but they weren't just rock. They glowed blue, so bright they almost hurt my eyes.

The augers must have been scratching at the Heechee wall liner for hours. They had actually worn pits into it.

We looked down, and we could see the round bright blue eye of the tunnel wall staring up at us. She was a beauty, all ours.

Even then we didn't speak.

Somehow I managed to kick and wriggle my way through the drift to the crawl-through. I got the lock closed and sealed, after kicking a couple of cubic meters of rock outside. Then I began fumbling through the pile of refuse for the flame drills. Ultimately I found them. Somehow. Ultimately I managed to get them shipped and primed. I fired them, and watched the bright pot of light that bounced out of the shaft and made a pattern on the igloo roof.

Then there was a sudden short scream of gas, and a clatter as the loose fragments at the bottom of the shaft dropped free.

We had cut into the Heechee tunnel. It was unbreached and waiting for us. Our beauty was a virgin. We took her maidenhead with all love and reverence and entered into her.

XII

I must have blacked out again, and when I realized where I was I was on the floor of the tunnel. My helmet was open. So were the side-zips of my hotsuit. I was breathing stale, foul air that had to be a quarter of a million years old and smelled every minute of it. But it was air. It was denser than Earth normal and a lot more humid; but the partial pressure of oxygen was about the same. It was enough to live on, in any case. I was proving that by breathing it and not dying.

Next to me was Dorrie Keefer.

The blue Heechee wall light didn't flatter her complexion. At first I wasn't sure she was breathing. But in spite of the way she looked her pulse was going, her lungs were functioning, and when she felt me poking at her she opened her eyes.

"We made it," she said.

We sat there grinning foolishly at each other, like Hallowe'en masks in the blue Heechee glow.

To do anything more than that, just then, was quite impossible. I had my hands full just comprehending the fact that I was alive. I didn't want to endanger that odds-against precarious fact by moving around. But I wasn't comfortable, and after a moment I realized that I was very hot. I closed up my helmet to shut out some of the heat, but the smell inside was so bad that I opened it up, figuring the heat was better.

Then it occurred to me to wonder why the heat was only unpleasant, instead of instantly fatal. Energy transport through a Heechee wall-material surface is very slow, but not a quarter of a million years slow. My sad old brain ruminated that thought around for awhile and came up with a conclusion: At least until quite recently, some centuries or thousands of years, maybe, this tunnel had been kept cool. Automatic machinery, of course, I though sagely. Wow, that by itself was worth finding. Broken down or not, it would be worth a lot of fortunes. . . .

And that made me remember why we were there in the first place, and I looked up the corridor and down, to see what treasures were waiting there for us.

When I was a school kid in Amarillo Central my favorite teacher was a crippled lady named Miss Stevenson, and she used to tell us stories out of Bulfinch and Homer. She spoiled a whole weekend for me with the story of one Greek fellow who wanted to be a god. He was king of a little place in Lydia, but he wanted more, and the gods let him come to Olympus, and he had it made until he fouled up. I forget how; it had something to do with a dog, and some nasty business about tricking the gods into eating his own son. Whatever it was, they gave him solitary confinement for eternity, standing neck deep in a cool lake in hell and unable to drink. The fellow's name was Tantalus, and in that Heechee tunnel I had a lot in common with him. The treasure trove was there all right, but we couldn't reach it. We hadn't hit the main tunnel but a sort of angled, Thielly-tube detour in it, and it was blocked at both ends. We could peer past half-closed gates into the main shaft. We could see Heechee machines and irregular mounds of things that might once have been containers, now rotted, with their contents on the floor. But we hadn't the strength to get at them.

It was the suits that made us so clumsy. With them off we might have been able to slip through, but then would we have the strength to put them back on again in time to meet Cochenour? I doubted it. I stood there with my helmet pressed to the gate, feeling like Alice peering into her garden without the bottle of drink-me, and then I thought about Cochenour again and checked the time.

It was forty-six hours and some odd minutes since he had left us. He was due back any time.

And if he came back while we were here, and opened the crawl-through to look for us and was careless about the seal at both ends, twenty thousand millibars of poison gas would hammer in on us. It would kill us, of course, but besides that it would damage the virgin tunnel. The corrosive scouring of that implosion of gas might wreck everything.

"We have to go back," I told Dorrie, showing her the time. She smiled.

"Temporarily," she said, and turned and led the way.

After the cheerful blue glow of the Heechee tunnel the igloo was cramped and miserable, and what was worse was that we couldn't even stay inside it. Cochenour probably would remember to lock in and out of both ends of the crawl-through. But he might not. I couldn't take that chance. I tried to think of a way of plugging the shaft, maybe by pushing all the tailings back in again, but although my brain wasn't working very well, I could see that was stupid.

So we had to wait outside in the breezy Venusian weather, and not too much later, either. The little watch dial next to my life-support meters, all running well into the red now, showed that Cochenour should in fact have arrived by now.

I pushed Dorrie into the crawl-through, squeezed in with her, locked us both through, and we waited.

We waited a long time, Dorrie bent over the crawl-through and me leaning beside her, holding on to her and the tie-down clips. We could have talked, but I thought she was either unconscious or asleep from the way she didn't move, and anyway it seemed like an awful lot of work to plug in the phone jack.

We waited longer than that, and still Cochenour didn't come.

I tried to think things through.

There could have been a number of reasons for his being late. He could have crashed. He could have been challenged by the military. He could have got lost.

But there was another possibility that made more sense than all of them. The time dial told me he was nearly five hours late now, and the life-support meters told me we were right up against the upper maximum for power, near it for air, well past it for water. If it hadn't been for breathing the Heechee gases for a while, we would have been dead by then, and Cochenour didn't know about that.

He had said he was a bad loser. He had worked out an end-game maneuver so he wouldn't have to lose. I could see him as clearly as though I were in the air-body with him, watching his own clocks, cooking himself a light lunch and playing music while he waited for us to die.

That was no frightening thought; I was close enough

to it for the difference to be pretty much a technicality, and tired enough of being trapped in that foul hotsuit to be willing to accept almost any deliverance. But the girl was involved, and the one tiny little rational thought that stayed in my half-poisoned brain was that it was unfair for Cochenour to kill us both. Me, yes. Her, no. I beat on her suit until she moved a little, and after some time managed to make her move back into the crawl-through.

There were two things Cochenour didn't know. He didn't know we'd found breathable air, and he didn't know we could tap the drill batteries for additional power.

In all the freaked-out fury of my head, I was still capable of that much consecutive thought. We could surprise him, if he didn't wait much longer. We could stay alive for a few hours yet, and then when he came to find us dead and see what prize we had won for him, he would find me waiting.

And so he did.

It must have been a terrible shock to him when he entered the igloo with the monkey-wrench in his hand and leaned over me, and found that I was still alive and able to move, where he had expected only a well-done roast of meat. The drill caught him right in the chest. I couldn't see his face, but I guess at his expression.

Then it was only a matter of doing four or five impossible things. Things like getting Dorrie up out of the tunnel and into the airbody. Like getting myself in after her, and sealing up, and setting a course. All these impossible things, and one other, that was harder than all of them, but very important to me.

I totaled the airbody when we landed, but we were strapped in and suited up, and when the ground crews came to investigate, Dorrie and I were still alive.

XIII

They had to patch me and rehydrate me for three days before they could even think about putting my new liver in. In the old days they would have kept me sedated the whole time, but, of course, they kept waking me up every couple of hours for some feedback training on monitoring my hepatic flows. I hated it, because it was all sickness and pain and nagging from Dr. Morius and the nurses and I could have wished for the old days back again, except, of course, that in the old days I would have died.

But by the fourth day I hardly hurt at all, except when I moved, and they were letting me take my fluids by mouth instead of the other way.

I realized I was going to be alive for a while, and looked upon my surroundings, and found them good.

There's no such thing as a season in the Spindle, but the Quackery is all sentimental about tradition and ties with the Mother Planet. They were playing scenes of fleecy white clouds on the wall panels, and the air from the ventilator ducts smelled of green leaves and lilac.

"Happy spring," I said to Dr. Morius.

"Shut up," he said, shifting a couple of the needles that pincushioned my abdomen and watching the telltales. "Um." He pursed his lips, pulled out a couple of needles, and said:

"Well, let's see, Walters. We've taken out the splenovenal shunt. Your new liver is functioning well, although you're not flushing wastes through as fast as you ought to. We've got your ion levels back up to something like a human being, and most of your tissues have a little moisture in them again. Altogether," he scratched his head, "yes, in general, I would say you're alive, so presumably the operation was a success."

"Don't be a funny doctor," I said. "When do I get out of here?"

"Like right now?" he asked thoughtfully. "We could use the bed. Got a lot of paying patients coming in."

Now, one of the advantages of having blood in my brain instead of the poison soup it had been living on was that I could think reasonably clearly. So I knew right away that he was kidding me; I wouldn't have been there if I hadn't been a paying patient, one way or another, and though I couldn't imagine how, I was willing to wait a while to find out.

Anyway, I was more interested in getting out. They packed me up in wetsheets and rolled me through the Spindle to Sub Vastra's place. Dorrie was there before me, and the Third of Vastra's house fussed over us both, lamb broth and that flat hard bread they like, before tucking us in for a good long rest. There was only the one bed, but Dorrie didn't seem to mind, and anyway at that point the question was academic. Later on, not so academic. After a couple days of that I was up and as good as I ever was.

By then I had found out who paid my bill at the Quackery. For about a minute I had hoped it was me, quickly filthy rich from the spoils of our tunnel, but I knew that was impossible. We could have made money only on the sly, and we were both too near dead when we got back to the Spindle to conceal anything.

So the military had moved in and taken everything, but they had shown they had a heart. Atrophied and flinty, but a heart. They'd gone into the dig while I was still getting glucose enemas in my sleep, and had been pleased enough with what they found to decide that I was entitled to some sort of finder's fee. Not much, to be sure. But enough to save my life. It turned out to be enough to pay off the loosely secured checks I'd written to finance the expedition, and surgical fee and hospital costs, and just about enough left over to put a down payment on a Heechee hut of our own.

For a while it bothered me that they wouldn't tell me what they'd found. I even tried to get Sergeant Little-knees drunk when she was in the Spindle on furlough. But Dorrie was right there, and how drunk can you get one girl when another girl is right there watching you? Probably Eve Littlekness didn't know anyhow. Probably no one did except a few weapons specialists. But it had to be something, because of the cash award, and most of all because they didn't prosecute for trespass on the military reservation. And so we get along, the two of us. Or three of us.

Dorrie turned out to be good at selling fire pearls to the Terry tourists, especially when her pregnancy began to show. She kept us in eating money until the high season started, and by then I found I was a sort of celebrity, which I parlayed into a bank loan and a new airbody, and so we're doing well enough. I've promised that I'll marry her if our kid turns out to be a boy, but as a matter of fact I'm going to do it anyway. She was a great help, especially with my own private project back there at the dig. She couldn't have known what I wanted to bring back Cochenour's body for, but she didn't argue, and sick and wretched as she was, she helped me get it into the airbody lock.

Actually, I wanted it very much.

It's not actually a *new* liver, of course. Probably it's not even second-hand. Heaven knows where Cochenour bought it, but I'm sure it wasn't original equipment with him. But it works. And bastard though he was, I kind of liked him in a way, and I don't mind at all the fact that I've got a part of him with me always.

1972 SELECTIONS FROM
THE PUBLISHER OF THE BEST
SCIENCE FICTION IN THE WORLD

1971 SELECTIONS FROM THE PUBLISHER OF THE BEST SCIENCE FICTION IN THE WORLD